These readers enjoyed LEGEN
what th.

The most amazing thing about this novel is it allows the reader to see African Americans in a different light. These four, nerdy, brainy, and quirky kids are superheroes in every sense of the word. Parents will love this book because there is so much diversity and acceptance in the group of friends, which will teach a valuable lesson. The author managed to capture the teenagers' personal lives in the mix of all the adventure, which was a great attention keeper in between all the adventures. [...] This is a recommended read for all cultures, races, and ages.

-Revues Galore, www.kanepresents.com

It's very difficult to write Young Adult fiction. The difficulty only increases when you add elements of science fiction and fantasy to the mix. M. Haynes, a Mississippi native, accomplishes this feat handily. [...] While the personalities of the lead characters are sometimes sketches, the strength of the novel is Haynes' ability to move the story along. He loves action and confrontation. Witness this: "The Silver Man and Master Rackson were in a dead beat battle on the first floor. The Silver Man was busy trying to smash Master Rackson with one of his hands currently shaped like a mallet, but the surprisingly nimble spell caster dodged every swing." Impassioned, exciting, and well-conceived, the novel is a marvelous achievement.

-Robert Fleming, African-American Literary Book Club (AALBC)

Read on and form your own opinions and don't forget to leave a review!

Age of Redd Vol. I:

LEGEND OF THE

ORANGE SCEPTER

M. HAYNES

CONTENTS

CONTENTS

Elementals

Acknowledgments

To my parents Thomas and Tawanna: Thank you for nurturing my geeky soul through it all.
To Kenny & Stephanie: Thank you for your strenuous edits, long conversations and constant encouragement and critique.
To the countless students, teachers and friends: Thank you for putting up with my constant talk about this book; your annoyance was not in vain.

This book is dedicated to all the geeky kids who look at their favorite books, comics, games and shows and don't see themselves. You too can be super.

Age of Redd Vol. I:

LEGEND OF THE

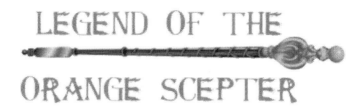

ORANGE SCEPTER

M. HAYNES

Test Day

"Name the four Mystics and their values."

"Ummm…okay. Sylver is all about order and laws, Redd is brainpower, Bleu was spirituality and Golde was curiosity."

"Good! Okay next part. How do these values relate to the four continents of Colorius?"

"Well we know that we Reddians are naturally more intellectual. The Bleusians have deep connections with religion and nature…I know that the Sylvanians had the most powerful monarchy and army on the planet and…umm…oh! Golde-lings are really magical."

"Man you got it. Why am I going through all of this with you again?"

"Because this history test is our final!" Morgan Peters said. He sat up in his bed staring in disbelief at Donald Henton, who sat at the desk in the corner of the room. Morgan had been out of school for the past week because of the contagious spots that dotted his body, and Don had predictably volunteered to pick up his homework assignments.

The two boys had known each other for five years, and over the course of that time they had bonded together quite strongly. Their similar levels of intellect and love of all things comic books, video games and cartoons had overpowered their differences in age, skin color, and build (Don was a year older, light skinned and chunkier than his skinny, more pale skinned companion), allowing them to remain such good friends for so long.

"Well, yeah but…" Don started.

"No buts! I *have* to pass this test; I can't afford to mess anything up! Give me more questions," he said impatiently.

"Okay fine. In their travels across the universe to study different life forms the Mystics found one planet in particular to model Colorius—"

"Wasn't it called Earth?"

"Yep. Now how did the first inhabitants come to Colorius?" Don asked.

"The Mystics brought a bunch of people to Colorius once they first made it. The original people from Earth brought a lot of their customs and began life on the planet as we know it." Morgan's response was practically word for word out of the textbook, but it was enough to satisfy Don. He put down his notes and started looking in the book for a new question.

"Okay! Here's one you should definitely know," he looked up at him and started laughing once he saw what he was up to. Morgan had tried to scratch one of the bright red spots on his arm, but the oven mitts his father had taped to his hands kept him from doing so. He sighed and motioned for Don to continue.

"In addition to the vast differences in locales and a few other small things, Colorius has one other fundamental difference between it and the planet it is based off of; what is the difference?" Don peered up from the textbook to hear Morgan's answer.

"Err...is there a multiple choice?" Mo said.

Don looked shocked. "Oh come on. Seriously?" Morgan shrugged and Don started shaking his head. He picked up his notes and started reading "...'the Elementals'-"

"Oh!" Morgan exclaimed.

"-'are groups of individuals with the power to control not only basic elements, but also lesser known powers.' What are the twenty elements the Elementals have the power to control?"

"Ice, Light, Darkness, Water, Chaos, Cosmic, Air, Earth, Fire, Nature, Psy, Electricity, Sync, Spirit, Sight, Sound, Ki...Beast, Morph, and..." Morgan started to draw a blank.

Don sighed. "I really need you to remember this part," he said. "The last one is Time, by the way," he picked back up his textbook and read another passage.

"'Though there are quite a few people all over the world with varying special abilities, only the Elementals have control over as many various powers and only they will grow in power to fully manipulate the elements.
Their advanced endurance, stamina and agility also aid them in fulfilling their divine duty to serve the people of
Colorius, and their fame has made generation after generation of Elementals both legendary heroes and major
celebrities.' How many generations of Elementals have there been?"

"Well, I'm sure that the book says four but we know it's five now," Morgan explained.

"Right. Well, right about the book. I wonder would Mrs. Summers mark your answer wrong if you did say five? If she did you could just show her your powers and-"

"Shhhh!!!" Morgan snapped. He looked around his bedroom as if he expected some alarm to go off.

Don frowned at him. "You mean to tell me you haven't told your Dad yet? Morgan...it's been almost four months..."

"I'm gonna tell him..." Morgan said quietly.

"You know that being an Elemental is nothing to be ashamed of right? 'The Elementals have protected Colorius from threats both from and to its people since the planet's creation. When the Mystics sense a substantial enough threat looming in the future of Colorius, one of them chooses ten children and blesses them with Elemental powers, so that they may learn to control their powers and use them to fulfill their destiny.' You've been given a divine blessing!" Don contested.

"Doesn't feel like it..." said Morgan. He still would trade his powers in a moment for the level of intellect that Don had.

Don knew how Morgan felt and decided to not push the subject. "Well, here are your notes. You can study some more if you want, but I think you've got it. I'm going to head home; my folks are probably waiting on me. When will you be back at school?"

Morgan looked a little off put by Don's harshness, but he knew it would pass. "I think this stuff is clearing up, so maybe on Monday? I should try to milk it longer though, isn't the test then?"

"That's what Mrs. Summers said when I was in her office, so maybe you should take that extra day." Don began packing up his textbooks. "Are you going to help your Dad and Lauryn take the Guardroid to Grandia this weekend?"

Morgan shook his head. "No, I probably won't be well by then. Besides, I'd rather take the test than do all the news stuff. They can have it. Thanks though Don. See you tomorrow?"

"Yep, later," Don closed Morgan's door behind him and yelled downstairs to Prof. Peters that he was leaving. The inventor didn't hear him, and instead kept working in his lab.

Professor Henry Peters was one of the brilliant minds common to Redd Continent. He had gained notoriety in his country, most specifically in his hometown of Rumas, as a guest lecturer at both of the huge city's universities and its lower level schools. He, his son Morgan and Don all worked in Prof. Peters' lab to create objects that would improve the lives of the people of Colorius. Today, he and one of his older inventions, an android named Lauryn, were busy putting the finishing touches on what was Prof. Peters' newest invention.

Clad in his buttoned up white lab coat and black rubber gloves, Prof. Peters scratched the bald spot of his head and stepped back to inspect his now finished creation. He grinned with satisfaction before he addressed his assistant.

"Lauryn, kindly hand me that photograph, will you, dear?" Prof. Peters asked.

"Sure, here you are," Lauryn handed the professor the item he requested and gazed upon his finished work. Lauryn began rolling down her sleeves as she reached for the photograph the professor spoke of: an old snapshot of two women embracing. Lauryn's long dirty blonde tresses and petite shape matched one of the women in the photo, just as the taller, blonder and shapelier image of the android in front of them matched the other woman. The two women in the photograph; Prof. Peters' wife Lauren and her best friend Adrian, were both deceased, and following his wife's death the grief stricken professor sought to ease his pain with a new companion, the android Lauryn.

Despite her mechanical makeup, Lauryn was seen as much more than an android to Prof. Peters and Morgan. She shared a vast knowledge of both men and their skin tone, making many who didn't know the truth believe that she was the professor's new wife.

She herself didn't object to that assumption, since she loved being able to care for the two men, and together the three of them made a loving, if not unusual, family. It was during a visit the family took to the rich northern land known as Grandia that the president of that country discovered the existence of Prof. Peters' android creation, and requested a special one just for him.

"She's perfect…she looks just like her," Prof. Peters said, stepping back to compare the android and the picture. An Adrian android to protect the president of Grandia just seemed fitting, he had thought.

"She's a perfect copy of the original. I should know," Lauryn laughed, glancing at the photo as well. "I'm sure Hammock will love her."

After hearing about Lauryn's functions Hammock requested an android that would be a guard for him; something inconspicuous and unintimidating, but powerful enough to be trusted with the life of one of the most powerful men on the continent. If Prof. Peters could create such an android; it would mean vast riches for the professor and his son, and mass producing of the androids as well as any of the professor's other inventions in an upscale factory paid for by the government.

So for the last five months Prof. Peters stretched himself to a breaking point to fulfill the president's wishes. He created an android that looked like a normal woman, but was armed with supreme strength, powerful laser based attacks, incredible resilience and high intellect. Now that the long process of perfecting her was finally over, he was ready to be delivered the following weekend.

"I think I'll call her…Adrienne. It only seems fitting; you know?" Prof. Peters shook the photograph to enforce his point.

"I bet the real Adrian would've gotten a kick out of this…" the professor chuckled to himself quietly. "Maybe you two can become friends?" He turned to look at Lauryn.

"Maybe," Lauryn smiled warmly. "I'll be sure to look her up if I'm ever in Greater Grandia. But in the meantime, why don't you go to bed? You know you will have a long day ahead of you tomorrow."

"You're right...tomorrow will be filled with plenty of publicity and questions, pictures and handshaking. Maybe I should make an android modeled after myself to do all the boring work for me," Prof. Peters suggested.

"Maybe, but later, go get some rest," Lauryn pressed.

"Alright fine, to bed I go. You should power down as well, you will have to do all of this with me tomorrow. We should both go upstairs," Prof. Peters turned off the lights, but not before he got a glimpse of what looked like someone crouching in the corner. He blinked, but saw nothing else.

He shook off what he figured was his eyes playing tricks on him, and he and Lauryn left his lab and went upstairs to bed.

The lab was quiet for only a few moments. From the corner of the room a rather short dark skinned woman in purple appeared seemingly out of pure darkness. She waved her hand towards another corner of the room, and her companion: a fearful looking light skinned man wearing all black emerged as if he stepped from behind a veil. "I thought they'd never leave!" the woman complained.

The male grunted as he struggled to get up from his hiding spot. "Are we sure this will work?" he asked his sister.

"It hurts me that you doubt me. Of course it will! Have I ever steered you wrong?" she asked. Her brother shook his head.

"No you haven't. Well, guard the door, I don't want them coming back down here while I'm working," The man pulled some tools from his belt and stooped down to open the android's chest cavity.

"Are you sure you know what you're doing?" the sister asked, peering down at him.

"It hurts that you doubt me, have I ever steered *you* wrong?" As soon as the words left his lips, he had opened the android. He removed the programming disk inside and replaced it with his own.

"Okay, now I just need to rewire a couple more things and boot her up for a second. If I've done this right, when they fire up this android tomorrow she's gonna make sure that people all over the world will tremble at the thought of the Pru Empire!" he exclaimed, looking happily at his sister. She grinned back at him.

"It's good to know all that schooling actually did some good," she patted the man on his shoulder. "Do your worst…it's time they remembered who we are…"

The Tyranny of A.G

Three Months Later

"Stand down, civilian! You are in a restricted area!" one of the three shining "male" androids barked at the young man standing in front of them. Their bald heads and silver frames shone in the bright afternoon sunlight; clashing with their humanlike features and voices. The brown skinned Reddian teenager turned around to look at them. He ran his fingers through his red hair before addressing the metal men who had stopped his walk back to the city.

"And here I thought we were still free to go wherever we pleased?" he wiped the crumbs from his lunch off of his mouth. "A guy can't walk home after lunch? Or is A.G. against fast food now too?"

"Do not speak of Queen A.G. in such a manner, civilian!" another of the androids snapped. He pushed the teen to emphasize his point, making him stumble off of the sidewalk. "Repeat: Leave this restricted area, or we shall have to exercise force..." the three androids surrounded the teen and all raised their left hands, sending the civilians who were around the boy scattering across the street. From the tips of the androids' fingers came a slight whirring sound, and the clear circles in the palms of their hands began to glow golden; a surefire sign that they were preparing to fire the laser blasts they were notorious for. What his attackers didn't know, however was that this was no ordinary civilian. They were dealing with the teenaged Elemental named Derren Lee.

"Civilian refuses to comply with demands!" The third android called, looking at the other two. Derren stepped a little further back while the androids kept their hands trained on him.

"FIRE!!" The lead android called. Just as the laser blasts left the palms of their hands, Derren aimed his own hands on the ground below him. He concentrated, and released a powerful burst of fire energy that propelled him off the ground and into the air. The two androids that were at his sides when he was on the ground missed their target and hit each other; their laser attacks tore through their metallic exteriors and caused them to shut down almost immediately. The third android could only watch as Derren returned to the ground and pitched fire at him as well. The android stumbled backwards from the force of Derren's flames, but tried to fire his laser blast again. Derren dodged the blasts and aimed his attacks first at the android's laser hand until he was able to knock it off. Derren continued to pelt the android with fire until the intense heat blew the stunned android's chest plate off, causing it to malfunction and shut down like the others.

"Stupid scraps." Derren remarked, kicking a piece of metal that came off one of the androids.

Derren, or De as his friends called him, was the newest member of the fifth generation of Elementals, meaning that he had been chosen by the Mystic Redd to carry on the tradition of the name. Like most Elementals, after his 13th birthday his latent powers came to life, and he need only experience a period of emotional (or physical, in some cases) trauma to be able to utilize his powers to protect himself and those he loves. Though he has only had his powers for a year, he is already well on his way to becoming a powerful Elemental, able to use his control of fire to defeat any threat that comes his way.

The people who had fled from De's confrontation with the androids cheered at him from across the street, and he waved back at them. He kept looking around the area as the small crowd began to disperse and couldn't help but wonder why the androids were so adamant about him leaving. He looked around Rumas and saw nothing out of the ordinary: the gigantic buildings were pretty much untouched, the streets were busy as usual, and the back road that led to the suburb of Cirix was as lonely as it always was. There was no reason for the androids to be so upset about him walking around the outskirts of town, so he decided to forget it and head back to Rackson Manor; his fellow Elementals and their teachers were waiting for him.

The young Fire Elemental continued his walk from his favorite restaurant and passed by the now normal group of people with their picket signs claiming that A.G. was the repayment for the people of Colorius' sins, and how she would destroy them all on his way to Rackson Manor. They yelled at passersby in cars and on foot, with De being no exception.

"Repent!" They yelled. "The end is upon us!" "You will all be judged!"

De shook his head. Ever since A.G. had gained control of the country, people had become very adamant about pushing the blame for her existence on others. It made sense, since someone had to be at fault for the demented creation that had ruined and taken so many lives from the people of the Great

Lands. De just wasn't so sure that the people at fault were the other people of the country.

He stopped once more, taking a moment to look at the gigantic screen atop the Rumas news station. "...meanwhile A.G. continues her seemingly never-ending conquest of the Great Lands. We still have yet to hear from our sister station in Rivera ever since A.G.'s androids were spotted in the quaint river town..."

The dark skinned woman on the screen with a serious expression and an even more serious bun spoke solemnly about the situation, trying her best to seem calm through all of this. De sighed and kept walking through the city streets, passing more buildings and the occasional person with a cardboard sign. "A.G. destroyed my home" and "Androids took my family" many of the signs said. De shuddered every time he saw signs like the last one; he knew all too well what A.G. and her forces were capable of.

Finally, De arrived at his destination; behind a large iron gate and at the end of a winding road to the top of a hill sat the huge and antique mansion of the Rackson siblings Matthew and Rose. They were older Elementals from the previous generation who took the time to instruct De, Maurice Black, Rodrik Reno, and Morgan Peters, who the collective group called Mo, how to properly use their powers.

De reached the end of the path and knocked on the oak front doors. He faintly heard a voice from the inside call "I'm coming!" and sure enough, the door opened and he looked down and saw Maurice Black, M for short.

Even though the top of the tiny Elemental's bushy black afro barely touched De's chest, it was M's attitude that made the electricity wielder dangerous. M was the youngest of the group at only thirteen years old, had a skin color to match his last name and was far scrawnier than any of his teammates (except possibly Mo). Despite all of this, M was the first of his comrades to meet and train with the Racksons and had taken it upon himself to become leader of the rag tag group. M had opened the door and scowled at De.

"Fix your face, little guy" De said, patting the top of M's hair. "It might get stuck that way." He walked around M and into the foyer of the mansion. A large winding double staircase took up most of the area, and the rooms on either side of the stairs showed the true girth of the manor. The first floor had the living room, a bathroom and a spare bedroom on one side and a kitchen, dining room, and a laundry room on the other. M glared at De's back as his comrade walked deeper into the foyer.

"You should worry less about my expressions and more about how your face will look when I rearrange it." M snarled. M had a shaky but friendly relationship with both Mo and Rod, but when De came around and his headstrong personality clashed with M's controlling one, they were destined to not get along.

"I'm sure it will look just fine," De responded. He turned around towards M when he heard no sounds in the hallway. "Is everyone downstairs already?"

"No, they're all upstairs in Master Rackson's study, waiting on him and Don to come back," M replied.

Despite not being an Elemental himself and being older than all of them, Don was still good friends with the others. He often helped out during training exercises and even sat in on educational lessons. He came almost as a packaged deal with Mo, but thankfully his enthusiasm for the team and skill as an engineer made him a valuable ally.

"Well, I guess we should join them," De said as he started up the stairs.

"You think?" M rolled his eyes in De's direction and followed him to the second floor. Instead of continuing to the left where Master Rackson's bedroom, the sun room, and the stairs to the attic were, they took a quick turn to the right side of the second floor to the three other bedrooms, the path to an outside balcony, and their destination: Master Rackson's huge study. De pushed open the double doors and saw that Rose Rackson and Rod Reno were already waiting for them inside.

"It took you two long enough. We heard you guys downstairs arguing forever." Rose turned her head away from a large window and towards the two boys. With her long blonde curls and the light from outside bouncing off her peach colored skin, Rose Rackson carried an almost otherworldly appearance befitting to the type of power she wielded. She stood near one end of the long table in the room, and placed her arm on an armchair near the window as she smiled at the two young boys.

Rose Rackson, though in her early 40s, often gave the impression that she believed she was still half her age. Even her attire backed this up; as the belly shirt and low rise jeans she wore revealed what looked to be a navel piercing. Her Elemental power to channel energy from the sun and use cosmic forces to power her fighting skills however, was quite well honed from her years of experience.

"You be arguing like you married or something. Something you need to tell us?" Rod's eyebrows lifted as he talked. Rod leaned back in his chair at the opposite end of the table, feet on the table and back on one of the many bookshelves in the room. The muscles in his dark (he was a shade darker than M) arms and legs flexed as he rocked himself forward and backward in his chair.

M went to sit down a chair beside Rod. "No, we'll leave the secret love affairs to you and your buddy Mo,"

He teased. Rod pushed M's chair, making him stumble a bit as he went to sit down.

"Aye don't play with me like that," Rod's outburst only made De laugh, and he went to sit down in a chair near Rose.

"He was just joking man, don't shoot him over it," De grinned.

"Why everybody gotta think I'm gonna shoot somebody? I'm reformed," Rod looked around seriously.

"You don't even believe that," M watched Rod to see his next reaction, but his friend simply laughed.

"Yeah, you're right. But I can't shoot anybody. I'm not even supposed to be holding nothing for a while," He explained.

The Water Elemental Rodrik Reno was one of the two founders of the locally infamous Black City street gang: the Heat Boyz. At the age of thirteen he and his best friend Jay were in charge of a bunch of other kids that built a reputation on getting into fights, selling all types of illegal substances, and stealing from stores and people to get the things they wanted out of life. No one dared to cross them until one night the gang was finally broken up by the police. Rod eluded them, but was caught stealing a few weeks later. Now two years older and not much wiser, he has been put on parole and through a series of other events he ended up being forced to check in with the Racksons to avoid being locked up like Jay was.

Rose turned back to the window when something caught her eye. "There's Matty and Don. I sure hope they have good news this time..." she said.

Rod shook his head, making the beads at the end of his braids clatter against his neck. "I doubt it. Androids have started popping up here; things can't be getting better."

Sadness raced across Rose's face as she turned to the others again. "If our Elemental generation was still active, we could have teamed up and taken down A.G. quickly. Now, we're here sending the kids to live with Mom and Dad until we can help you guys take care of things...stuff is just so different."

Rose and her older brother Matthew Rackson's generation of Elementals; called Generation Immortal, were chosen by the Mystic Golde to face evil over twenty years ago. Rose Rackson, a Cosmic Elemental, and Matthew Rackson, a Chaos Elemental, fought alongside their eight teammates to take down the Pru Empire and stop the Sylvanian monarchy from destroying their country. Now their generation had lost touch and Matthew and Rose live their adult lives in their parents' mansion with Matthew's three-year-old son and Rose's two-year-old daughter.

The entire room tensed up instantly the moment Master Matthew Rackson walked in. Though he was only three years older than his sister, Master Rackson carried himself with the air of authority that his sister could only hope to have. Perhaps it was his legendary skill at magic and his ability to utilize it to hex other people and objects, or perhaps it was the fact that even with his back-length blonde ponytail and clothed in a deep purple cloak that draped over his peach colored (but slightly sagging) skin the middle-aged master's very presence screamed serious business. When Master Rackson sat down at the head of the long table in his study, Rod took his feet off the table, Rose sat down in a seat, and M and De stopped bickering to listen intently to what Master Rackson's had to say.

"Good afternoon, everyone," Master Rackson said. After a canopy of responses, he continued. "Donald will be upstairs in a minute; Morgan was walking up the path. He will be waiting on him."

"The guy can't walk upstairs by himself?" Rod asked before he could stop himself. M stomped on his foot a little too late.

"I'm sure the two of them are discussing matters that our tiny minds cannot hope to understand," Master Rackson laughed.

"Yeah right," Rod said. He held back his choice words towards M when the two people they were just discussing walked into the room.

The usually jubilant Don looked especially somber as he and his companion sulked into their seats: Don beside M and Mo beside Rose. Don answered the question on everyone's minds.

"Prof. Peters has been arrested. They're saying that he is to blame for everything A.G.'s done."

"What? They can't possibly think Henry planned for all this?" Rose asked. She leaned over to try and comfort Mo, who was still silent.

"They're saying that because A.G. was his invention, he has to assume responsibility for all the destruction and deaths she caused," Don replied. Mo sniffed loudly and Rose continued to rub his shoulders.

"Sounds like the cops," Rod shook his head. "Folks are upset because the police can't do anything about A.G., so to make it seem like they're tryna stop her, they arrest the Prof and blame everything on him."

"It always surprises me how well you know how police think," De said, looking across at him in awe.

"When you live like I do you can't help but pick up a few things," Rod shrugged.

"Where is Henry now?" Master Rackson asked.

This time it was Mo who answered. Unlike the other Elementals Mo was very quiet in most group settings. His social skills were lacking from years of self-inflicted seclusion, and even though he had joined the "team," it was obvious he was much more interested in being an intellectual like his father and best friend than training his Elemental powers, which he still had not told is father about. He shook his head to move the blonde bangs from his eyes before speaking, and when he did his high voice was raspy from crying.

"They took him to the prison! They said that he can await trial there, they didn't even mention a bail, so I know they're going to keep him there forever!" the Ice Elemental shook his head pitifully and slumped further into his seat. "It's just not right, do they really think my dad *wanted* A.G. to do all that stuff? Do they think that *he* wanted to take over the world?!" He looked around the table for an answer, but when none came he buried his
face in his hands and let the tears flow again. Rod looked away from him while Rose and Don continued to try to be comforting. M and De exchanged worried looks, and Master Rackson sat back in his chair, letting this news settle in the minds of his students as he replayed the scenes of how they got to this point in the first place.

The morning after Prof. Peters finished his work on the Adrienne android, he and Lauren traveled to the capital city of Grandia; Greater Grandia. Just as Prof. Peters had guessed he and Lauryn spent the better part of the morning talking with President Hammock and several reporters who were overly excited about the idea of this prominent city having new security guards. They barely had time to breathe, let alone check out the Adrienne android before the unveiling that evening.

When five o'clock finally rolled around President Hammock held a ceremony to demonstrate the efficiency of the publicly funded Guardroids. President Hammock activated Adrienne, but instead of responding to the president's request to subdue his "attacker" (a chubby man in an over the top costume), the android screamed "LONG LIVE THE PRU EMPIRE!" and slaughtered the man, President Hammock, some members of his cabinet and quite a few people gathered to watch the display with her powerful laser blasts. The android's considerable power made her untouchable to even the finest of Greater Grandia's police force; no one could stand in her way.

Prof. Peters and Lauryn escaped the bloodbath and returned home as quickly as they could. Word of the android's rampage in Greater Grandia spread like wildfire over Redd Continent as the machine left a bloody trail of death and destruction as she met up with two humans outside of Grandia, and the three of them made their way from the northernmost tip of the continent southward.

The three of them, armed with Adrienne's raw strength, the intellectual prowess of the female and the technological intellect of the male, were unstoppable, and the entire continent was forced to watch what was just the beginning of Adrienne's reign of terror.

A week and a half later the "Terrible Trio," as they came

to be called, finally ended their journey when they arrived in the southernmost country on Redd Continent: Phorbes. Reports began to fly in about the three of them storming a historical temple and attempting to steal a legendary treasure known as the Orange Scepter. Rumors ranged from Adrienne stealing the scepter and destroying it, to her massacring the monks inside, to them never having made it to the temple in the first place. The only certainty was that the two human conspirators were temporarily apprehended before they escaped imprisonment and went into hiding.

Adrienne, however, continued her takeover on the main front. With rumors of her having the Orange Scepter (true or not) she was able to begin her journey to world domination. Adrienne's human companions had succeeded in reprogramming all of the other already made Guardroids, so with her army of over 200 super powered androids she succeeded in taking over the Great Lands, Grandia, and the Underground Kingdom. With the three largest countries of the continent now under her control, Adrienne renamed herself A.G., standing for Android Goddess, and claimed that the rest of Colorius would soon belong to the Pru Empire, and by extension, her.

Once she had killed the President of the Great Lands and had taken over the monarchy of the Underground Kingdom, it was hard to dispute this boast. With A.G. in control, she forced the factory workers in Greater Grandia to continue manufacturing the Guardroid line, making them all into androids with most of the same abilities as her. Though these mass produced androids didn't share all of A.G.'s power or resilience, they were still strong enough to help their leader turn the once peaceful and thriving land into a place of fear and terror. The androids created in the Greater Grandia factory spread to the Great Lands and the Underground Kingdom, erecting other factories so that more and more of them could be created, further solidifying A.G.'s takeover.

Citizens all over the continent spent their days terrified that the androids may come knocking at their door to force them to go work at one of A.G.'s factories, or that they would just flat out kill them for whatever reason. The land tried its best to live life as normally as possible, but the fear of A.G. was crippling its livelihood. Schools began closing (though the Elementals in particular had no objection to that), travel to and from these three countries was restricted severely, people disappeared left and right, and businesses closed their doors all over.

That had been enough for the Racksons to feel that they had to act.

By that time they had three new Elementals, and for three grueling months they trained them in the hopes that they would soon be able to take down A.G.

"With A.G. still forcing people to build her soldiers in the factories and things getting worse, I can't see the police releasing Prof. Peters anytime soon. Like Rod said, they have to make people feel like they're doing something. It makes sense," M pointed out despite Mo's continued cries.

"That's enough, Maurice. You're not helping, you should be consoling Morgan, not rationalizing the mistakes of others," Master Rackson said sternly. M looked away, embarrassed, and muttered "Sorry Mo," under his breath.

"So this is it, right? We're gonna go stomp out A.G. and get Mo's dad off the hook, right?" De asked excitedly.

"Not yet Derren, we still have preparations to make and

tactics to discuss before we can stand a chance against A.G.," Master said.

"Yea...we gotta move on," Mo said with some difficulty. "What did you guys find out, Don?" Don looked a little surprised at his best friend's bravado, but answered his question anyway.

"Well, Mr. Rackson and I found out that the androids are building a factory, here, in the city. Well, in Cirix anyway," Don said. The room exchanged glances at this revelation. Suddenly, the actions of androids that tried to force De away from the entrance to Cirix made sense.

Worry, anguish, and pure fear wiped over all of their faces, they all knew that this was bad news for their home, but De was the first to directly ask the question.

"So...if the factory is here...who will work in it?"

Rod barked out a laugh. "Isn't it obvious? Us...our families, our friends...A factory in Cirix would pull people from Rumas, Center City, probably even Black City into it if it's big enough. A.G.'s gonna come down here and send us all to the factory to keep making her bags of bolts," He laughed again and let his words take hold.

Master Rackson felt the gloom that hung heavy in the room and stood up. "Of course, this is something we cannot allow to happen. A.G. cannot be allowed to build another factory, not here," His voice rang with clarity over the room; the willingness even at his age to not lie down and take A.G.'s newest expansion was inspiring. "The factories A.G. already has have produced hundreds, maybe even thousands of the androids she uses to enforce her rule. Another one, especially one in the heart of our land will up that production even further. Our only option is to find some way to stop the construction of this factory. We will destroy this factory, and we will continue on to destroy the others, or risk being dragged off to one ourselves."

Training

"But didn't you say that we weren't ready to face A.G.? We can't go off trying to do something that may be suicide," M reasoned.

"No, I stated that we must prepare before we face A.G., and that we shall do," Master Rackson clarified. He motioned for Don to pick up the response, to which he let out a small "Oh…" and leaned up in his chair.

"The factory is still in its beginning stages; it could be weeks before it is operational-"

"So we have plenty of time right?" Rose interrupted

Don shook his head. "Not quite. If what I've learned about these factories is true, the androids only build the basic framework of it. They bring in humans to finish the factory and start building new androids inside of it. With the framework nearly complete, I'd guess that we have a week at the most."

"Oh…" Rose, chagrined, stopped trying to console Mo and leaned back in her seat.

"…Which means we have only a week's time to destroy the factory's framework. It will delay the building of a new factory, and hopefully send a message to A.G. and her forces. We will have to watch the factory closely, search for any weaknesses in its defense and in the factory itself. We will also have to spend the better part of this week training harder than ever to ensure that you all are able to take on the androids that will inevitably be there to defend the factory," Master Rackson said.

"Well that won't take long. I take out androids all the time, *I* have had plenty of training," M boasted, cutting his eyes at De. De shook his head.

"Problem?" M asked.

De continued to shake his head. "What makes you think that you don't need training like the rest of us?"

M smiled and leaned over to look closer at De. "Simple. I am the original member of this generation..." he began.

"...'the first person to begin training with the Racksons and therefore the leader.' The more you say that doesn't make it any more true," Rod finished. M opened his mouth to argue further, but Master Rackson raised his hand, causing silence to fall once more.

"Our time is too precious for arguments. Let us move to the training room, if we are to take out this factory being built, we must ensure that you all are able to do so," He said, and with a whirl of his cloak moved the short distance from his chair to the door.

"Umm, Master Rackson?" Mo looked over at his teacher.

Master Rackson turned from the door to look at him. "Yes Morgan?"

"Is it alright if I skip training today? I...really don't feel up to it..." he said quietly.

Master Rackson sighed. "Morgan...we are getting to the point where each lesson is vitally important. I understand that you have been through a lot today, but-"

"Oh Matty let him go," Rose interrupted. "He just found out his dad is in jail indefinitely. He probably wouldn't be any good in practice anyway. Remember when we were on Sylver Continent? How you felt the first time Emilia—"

Master Rackson gave her a mean look, and she stopped talking and started laughing instead. Master Rackson turned slightly red, and turned back to Mo. "Very well, Morgan. Take this day to get your emotions in order. I expect to see you tomorrow."

"I'll be here," Mo said. He got up from his chair and headed to the door.

"I'll walk down with you, Mo," Don offered.

Mo nodded. "See you tomorrow guys," he said and was gone.

"The rest of you," Master Rackson said, looking at De, M and Rod. "Follow me."

The collective group followed Master Rackson down towards the basement of the huge manor. When the Racksons' grandparents built their mansion, they made the basement into a nearly indestructible bunker to protect their family should the effects of the Global War ever come to Rumas. When the war ended and the mansion was passed down, Master Rackson and Rose were able to use the bunker as a training facility to teach the new Elementals how to control their powers without fear of any lasting damage. As each of them came into the Racksons' lives they all began training their abilities in preparation for the time when they would be most needed.

"I will never get over how huge this place is," Don said. He met them on the first floor after Mo left and now walked with Rose behind the trio of new Elementals and their teacher. They all entered a door between the double stairs in the foyer and began walking down a stairway into the basement. The bunker, built to withstand any type of attack, was easily as large as a football field and rested at the bottom of these stairs.

"Yeah it's crazy how much money our grandparents had to blow on this place," Rose admitted to Don. She opened the huge steel door at the end of the stairs (the lock had been disabled long ago) and they walked into the basement bunker.

Master Rackson strode deeper into the gigantic underground room, and the motion activated lights switched on inside of it as he walked. The others stood in the center watching him head to the other side of the room. At the far end of it was a closed off section that resembled a small home. This "house" was no doubt designed to be a living quarters should the Racksons' grandparents ever need to live in the bunker for a while. Nowadays, the "house" was used for little more than storage by the Racksons currently living in the manor, and for the past year or so it has been where they kept the training equipment for the young heroes. Sure enough, Maser Rackson emerged from the house after a few moments dragging a very large chest.

"If you remember correctly," he said once he was near enough for the others to hear him. "I told you all about how many of the past generations made a habit of using their individual powers in conjunction with their allies to create devastating combination attacks." The three Elementals nodded. M took it a step further.

"Like how in the first generation, the Air and Water Elementals used their powers to create the storms that filled many of our lakes," he said.

"Correct Maurice," Master Rackson said. M smiled widely, while Rod muttered "Show off." De snickered.

"Today," Master Rackson continued, "You three will practice your own combination attacks. In order to bring down something as powerful as the factories A.G. is using to manufacture her androids, or the android queen herself, your individual powers will have to be augmented," he bent down to open the chest and pulled out what seemed to be a vaguely human shaped dummy covered in what looked like a coat of burgundy velvet.

"What is that?" De asked.

"Your opponent," Master Rackson said simply. He laid the dummy on the ground and stepped to the side. The three Elementals looked at each other and smiled.

"This won't be hard will it?" M said. "Well team, let's take out this dummy." The three of them approached the motionless dummy, and Master Rackson smiled. "Kareema Rhama Heximae!" he hissed, and his tried and true incantation sent forth a blast of purple, gold and red magical energy from his hands to the dummy. The second the energy touched the dummy, it leapt to its feet and balled up its "fists." Its blank head turned to each of its three attackers in turn.

"What the?!" Rod stopped where he was, as did the other two. They and Don looked to Master Rackson in surprise. Rose, however, just grinned.

"Surely you did not think that you would be fighting a lifeless dummy? The androids will be very mobile, as you will have to be when attacking the factories. Consider this dummy your real world practice," he walked back over to the chest and pulled a large stick from it. He handed it to the dummy, which swung the stick menacingly. "Now, attack as you will."

"Wait!" Rod said. "I, um, there's no water..." He said.

"You have not learned how to manipulate moisture in the air yet, Rodrik? We talked about you practicing outside of training," Master Rackson said. Rod looked away from him.

Rose ran to the house towards the back, and came back with a mop bucket full of liquid. "Here you go," she said.

"Thanks. Ok, we're ready now," Rod said, and the three Elementals rounded on the enchanted dummy.

Rod began the attack by sending the water from the bucket towards the dummy. The dummy was doused, but ran towards its attackers. De began throwing small fires at the dummy, causing Rod's water to dry up.

"No, Derren, you have cut off one of your comrade's weapons!" Master Rackson said.

The dummy swung the stick at De, who moved too slowly to avoid it and got hit hard. He nursed his side but ran from the dummy's continued swings. Rose ran around the dummy and the other Elementals and grabbed the bucket to go refill it.

M started shooting bolts of electricity at the dummy even as he laughed at its steady attacks towards De.

"Maurice, you should be aiding your teammate, not laughing at him!" Master Rackson barked. Rose returned with a now filled bucket, and Rod used the water inside of it to direct the dummy's attention away from De.

"Rodrik, you have to learn to conserve your water!" Master Rackson said as Rose grabbed the bucket to go refill it once again, muttering under her breath the whole way.

De decided to attack again; this time aiming for the dummy's legs as it walked towards Rod. M added to the onslaught by shooting a little electricity at it, making the flames grow a bit.

"Good, good! That is one combination, keep it up!"

M beamed at Master Rackson's compliment and shot more electric bolts at the dummy, but this time it was ready for them. It moved out of the way and the bolt hit De in the chest.

"OUCH!" the Fire Elemental groaned. He doubled over in pain.

"Sorry," M said smugly. He turned back to the dummy and continued trying to hit it with electricity, and Rod joined in the attack by using a very small amount of water to splash the dummy.

"Now you will have to use more water than *that*, Rodrik," Master Rackson said, choosing to ignore Rod's not so subtle eye roll. "Come on, think, how can you add to the combination?" he asked.

Rod seemed to take a moment to think, which was just long enough for the dummy to hit him with its stick as well. He got angry and shoved the dummy, which was a move not even the dummy seemed to expect. It fell on its back, and struggled to get up. All three Elementals laughed at its predicament. Even Don chuckled from behind Rose and Master Rackson, but neither of them smiled.

"Stop," Master Rackson said, and immediately the dummy went limp again and the boys stopped laughing. "This is no laughing matter, you three will have to learn how to work together to take down an enemy, you cannot simply take turns hitting a foe if you want to succeed in defeating A.G."

"I think we need to show them what we mean by combination attacks, Matty," Rose suggested. Master Rackson looked at his sister and nodded.

"Yes, I think we should. Stand back, you three," Master

Rackson said. The three quickly moved out of the way. "Are you ready?" Master Rackson asked.

Rose reached into her pocket and pulled out a hairband and used it to pull her hair back into a ponytail. "Of course I am; bring the thing to life already," she stretched her arms as she walked beside her brother.

"Very well," Master Rackson said. He yelled his magic words again and once again the dummy sprang to life, this time with its sights set on the Rackson siblings.

Despite their ages, the two Racksons moved surprisingly quickly when the dummy ran at them with its stick. Master Rackson dove to the dummy's side, while Rose engaged it in hand to stick combat. Rose's punches and kicks were powerful, but it seemed that the dummy was just as strong with its weapon. Eventually, Master Rackson sent more magical energy towards the dummy, this time aiming for its weapon. The shining light hit the stick and snatched it away from the dummy, giving Rose the advantage she needed to overpower the dummy.

"You see how we work together?" Master Rackson pointed out. He held the stick up for emphasis, but the dummy saw this and shoved Rose out of the way (it seemed to have picked up on this tactic from Rod) to chase after its lost weapon.

Master Rackson prepared for the dummy, and he and the thing began battling. The dummy threw punches and Master Rackson was able to use its own stick to distract it from Rose. She ran behind the dummy and also began fighting it, with the dummy surprisingly holding up against the both of them.

"How is it doing that? Isn't Master Rackson controlling it?" De asked.

"Not if it's enchanted. An object enchanted by a Chaos Elemental can act on its own accord if the Elemental is powerful enough to make it do so," M explained.

"Forget that, what is the thing *made* of? That's got to be the fifteenth time Rose has punched it and it's still going...make that sixteenth," Rod said, wincing at the painful looking beating the two Racksons were giving it.

"I was wondering that too," Don said. "It looks like the actual dummy is plastic, but whatever is covering it must be...oh!" he said suddenly. He pulled a notepad out of his pocket and scribbled something down on it. The others shrugged and continued watching the fight.

By now, Master Rackson and Rose were staring down the dummy from near the house at the back. Somehow it had wrestled its stick back and was nearer to the Elementals waiting for its opponents to make a move. The two siblings looked at each other and nodded. Master Rackson sent out another blast of magical energy, this time directly at Rose. The energy enveloped the Cosmic Elemental and lifted her off the ground. With surprising ease, he threw Rose directly at the dummy. She flew through the air, and despite the dummy swinging its stick at her, landed on top of it.

Rose laid on top of the dummy, and her weight pressed on the dummy more and more, making it impossible for the dummy to fight back; its stick rolled harmlessly across the floor. She got up and dusted herself off, leaving the now completely flat and stretched out dummy lifeless once again on the floor.

The three Elementals and Don erupted into applause, and Rose took a bow.

"How did you flatten that thing like that?" De asked. Behind him M rolled his eyes.

"As a Cosmic Elemental, and a good one at that, I have the ability to manipulate my own gravitational field. I can make myself light enough to float or heavy enough to crush most stuff. The dummy just happened to be most stuff," Rose explained. "Matty, of course, knows that and that's why he threw me at the dummy."

"Knowledge of your comrades' skills as well as your own will be vital to your success as Elementals. Only by understanding your abilities, your flaws, and your strengths will you truly be able to work together efficiently," Master Rackson said to the trio of Elementals. They all nodded and he continued. "Well, considering our opponent is out of commission, I think this would be a good time to adjourn for today. I would like you all to come back tomorrow having done some research on your elements to better be able to understand how to use them with your comrades' powers. I expect to see you all here with that information bright and early tomorrow," Master Rackson said, allowing the Elementals and Don to leave the bunker and head to their various homes.

Hard Work

The next morning De woke up to the sound of someone pounding on the manor's front door. Ever since he joined the Elementals, he had been living with the Racksons in one of their spare rooms. He was just wondering what sort of cool combination attacks he and his fellow Elementals could pull off when M walked into his room.

"This place is a mess," M commented, looking around the room. De didn't have many things, but everything he did have was sprawled around the room the Racksons were letting him live in.

"It's not a mess; it's exactly like I want it," De replied. He reached for his favorite muscle shirt, put it on, and hopped out of his bed.

"Do you have anything with sleeves on it?" M asked. In just the two weeks he had known De, he had already grown tired of seeing his budding biceps all the time.

"Sorry kid, we can't all be rocking the slim fit look," De laughed, poking M's scrawny chest.

"Shut up! I don't need to be huge anyway, I just need my powers," M pushed De's hand off of him and pouted for a moment. "You just hurry up and come down to the bunker," he said and walked out of the room. De continued to laugh as he put on a pair of pants for today's training.

By the time De got dressed and grabbed some food from the kitchen, Rod, Mo and Don had all arrived at the manor and were already downstairs in the bunker. De walked in, still chewing his breakfast as Don was speaking to the others.

Don reached into the large bag he brought with him and began pulling out clothes. "I call it Skin Armor," he said to De. "I was telling the others that after I realized that the dummy you guys fought yesterday was made of Crystanium, I had finally found the material I needed to make you guys some armor! I mean, I saw how much you got hurt from M's electricity," M made no effort to hide how proud he was of himself for being the inspiration behind this new wardrobe. "...and I know A.G. would be even stronger, so I figured if you had Crystanium clothes that wouldn't have happened," Don explained. He watched De feel the jeans he handed to him and continued.

"It's pretty resistant to regular wear and tear. It should be fire proof, water resistant, and pretty much able to withstand anything else you guys can throw at them. I tried to make them as close to what you guys would normally wear, so you can wear them whenever you want," Don finished.

De lifted the red sleeveless shirt that was his. It even bore a large flame on the front. "Cool!" he said, hurriedly taking off his own shirt to put on Don's Skin Armor. The others were a tad bit more respectful and waited until Rose had turned around before they put on their clothing.

"I like them." Rod said, pulling his jeans down so that they were off his waist. His black t-shirt was just big enough to make sure that most of his body was covered. "We only get one outfit?" he asked Don.

"Yeah, sorry. It was hard work making these last night, so I could only make all of you one outfit. I couldn't even make the Racksons one..." he said, looking apologetically at Master Rackson and Rose. They exchanged a glance and simply shrugged.

"Why don't you put yours on Mo?" M asked; his Skin Armor was the easiest to pick out since he was the only one with a blue jean vest to go with his long sleeved, fitted white shirt and khakis. "Go on, change out of that junk and see what Don made for you!"

"I already have mine on..." Mo said, gesturing at the purple and yellow plaid shirt and brown pants he was wearing.

"Oh..." M replied. He quickly looked away while Rod barely suppressed a laugh.

Master Rackson took control of the situation by changing the subject. "What combinations have you come up with?" he asked.

"Well, I know that with fire I kinda have to be careful when Rod or Mo are doing something," De began.

"Yes, this is correct. Morgan's ice based abilities cannot stand up to intense flames. However, by combining your abilities with Rodrik's you can do something fairly useful. Can you think of what a large amount of water and heat could create?" Master Rackson asked. De took a moment to think of the answer, but Rod beat him to it.

"Oh, steam!"

Master Rackson smiled. "Yes. Steam is an excellent smokescreen for quick getaways and can even sometimes be damaging. It may be very useful to you in the future. What else?"

"Well, electricity can spark fires to make them bigger, so I can help him a lot," M said, pointing at De. "Water also conducts electricity so Rod and I are more powerful together, but we knew that already," M said, thinking back to how when he and Rod first started training together they faced off with the Racksons.

"Good, good," Master Rackson seemed pleased. He turned to Mo. "Morgan have you put any thought to what you can do in combination with your teammates?"

"Umm...the only thing I could think of was how since I can't make my own ice yet I can use Rod's water right?" Mo said sheepishly.

"Yes. You and Rodrik are especially linked because of the closeness of your elements. You two make a great combination." Rod and Mo looked at each other; neither of them thought of themselves as a "good combination" with the other.

"It seems you have put some thought into what I have asked you to do. We will talk more about combination attacks later, but first we will train in sparring. If you are to be successful in fighting the android army A.G. has created, you must be trained in fighting opponents with powers not unlike your own. The androids, as you have no doubt seen, have heightened endurance much just as you do. Their laser attacks are also very powerful; I daresay they are stronger than the attacks you can muster now," he paused to allow them to protest this. Predictably, M muttered his disagreement and Rod rolled his eyes, but De and Mo simply listened on. "Your main advantage over them will then be the adaptability of your abilities and your agility. You will have to out maneuver and out think the androids in order to succeed. Hopefully, a battle here will teach you all to use your powers creatively and the ample space will teach you to maneuver."

Don and Rose pulled up two chairs from a corner of the room and sat down, preparing for Master Rackson's further instructions. The others anxiously waited to hear who their partners would be.

"Maurice, you will spar with Derren. Rodrik, you and Morgan will battle." Master Rackson turned around towards his sister and Don, and the latter got out of the chair he brought and sat on the floor to make room for the Elemental.

"In this sparring match no outside weapons are allowed," Master continued, glancing at Rod. Rod shrugged and took a silver and black weapon from his pocket and slid it across the floor towards Master Rackson. Mo looked from the firearm to Rod in utter terror. Rod shrugged.

"I won't inform anyone of that…" Master Rackson said, handing Rod's weapon to Rose. "The goal of this 'match' is to simply render your opponent unwilling to continue. Unwilling, not unable," Master Rackson added. He had no doubt seen the dangerous glares M and De had exchanged. "Remember, however, despite the outcome of the match you will all still be needed in our journey to reclaim the city and to clear Henry's name."

At his father's name Mo sighed sadly, causing Rod to loudly ask "Can I get a sparring partner who's not putting out more water than me?" Mo scowled at him, but saw Rod's "piece" on the floor beside Don and changed his expression quickly.

Master Rackson ignored him. "That reminds me," he said. He walked back to the house at the back of the bunker and returned with a much larger and fuller bucket of water. He pushed it in between Rod and Mo and returned to this seat. "Are you all ready?" All four Elementals nodded, never taking their eyes off their opponent.

"Ready..." Master Rackson called. They all tensed up for the coming battle.

"I'm going to show you what it takes to be on this team..." M taunted.

"...Set..."

"You're gonna show me that you don't have it?" De said, much to M's anger.

"GO!!!" Master Rackson called, and the battle was on.

M immediately raised his hands and released a bolt of electricity from them. However, De took Master Rackson's advice about maneuvering and leapt away from the attack. M continued his electrical attacks, making De run around the room to dodge them.

"Attack, De! Stop running!" Rose yelled.

De decided to just that. He spun around to face M, and as he spun, he kicked his foot in the Electric Elemental's direction, sending a burst of fire towards him. M wasn't expecting this, so the fire caught him in the stomach and made him double over in pain.

Luckily, Don's Skin Armor was indeed fireproof, and the attack caused no damage to his clothing.

"That's hot..." Rose said, eyeing the balls of flaming energy De launched at M. Master Rackson and Don stared at her. "What?" she asked, looking back at them. "It is hot; you guys aren't sweating?"

It seemed that De's heat was affecting Mo, as well. As Rod splashed him with the water from the bucket, he was unable to turn any of it into solid ice, and each time he tried he only made Rod splash him harder. The two went back and forth; with Mo trying to freeze the air around Rod, failing, and Rod using the water to splash Mo. Eventually Rod grew tired of this back and forth, and summoned all the water around the two of them and launched it in a continuous wave at Mo.

"I...can't....breathe..." Mo choked

"Well fight back then!" Rod taunted. He did not let up on poor Mo, and was using his other hand to recycle the water so that the Elemental barely got a moment of air in between waves. Poor Mo wouldn't be able to withstand this torture for much longer...

M was refusing to be beaten that easily. A well timed bolt of electricity struck De's left hand and freed M from the fiery barrage. It was now M's turn to overwhelm De with his powers...for all of fifteen seconds. De caught on to M's attack pattern quite quickly and used his powers to propel himself into the air.

The force of the propulsion sent a wave of fire all around De's launching point, and M had to practice his own dodging skills to avoid it.

The wave did however, connect with Rod, who yelled in shock and lost his focus on his attack on Mo.

This was all the opportunity Mo needed and used the break in heat to release a blast of chilling air towards Rod. He froze the water around Rod's hands and feet, effectively stopping his attack and Rod's movement.

"Go Mo!" Don leapt from the floor to cheer his best friend on.

Mo stood up and scooped some of the water on the floor around him in his hand. He froze the water in his hand,

and threw the newly formed block of ice at Rod. Rod winced but was forced to endure. Mo continued this ice tossing, much to Rod's anger.

"Alright bud!" Don was as excited as if he himself were beating Rod. This continued cheering proved to be a mistake, as when Mo smiled at his friend, he gave Rod the opportunity he needed. He moved his fingers a few inches and was able to bring enough rushing water to his hands to free them from the ice. He smashed his hands against the ice on his feet, freeing them. He grimaced through the pain in his hands, but his glare at Mo made it clear he would make the Ice Elemental pay for his torment.

"Pay attention, Morgan!" Master Rackson yelled, but it was too late. Rod was free and used the left over water around the two to return to drowning Mo.

"Bet you thought you were doing good, huh?" Rod gloated. "You ain't good enough, boy."

Mo tried to recover from this renewed attack, but the water was again proving to be too much. It looked like Mo might really lose this time; Master Rackson even rose from his seat to stop the sparring when Rod was struck again, this time by a bolt of electricity. Thanks to all the water around him, the electricity shocked Rod to his core. He fell down backwards, still jittery from his electric encounter. Mo began to laugh at Rod's predicament, but Rod was now fully focused on getting back at M. He waved his hand and sent some of the water rushing at M. The young teen was too busy dodging De's flames and trying to land his own attack to notice this sneak attack.

"Hey!" M yelled after the burst of water hit him. He tried to move his soggy afro out of his eyes and shot off a few blasts of electricity. Of course, since he was covered in the element that conducted electricity, all of M's attacks backfired and hit him. The electricity couldn't harm M, but as he was still blinded by his own hair when he ran around the room to locate his attacker he eventually bumped into De. De was too busy laughing at M, and didn't realize that the electricity around M would hurt him until it did. By this time Rod was crying laughing at his comrades, and De, embarrassed and angry, tried to start a blaze in his direction. Rod, having learned his lesson from previous attacks, dodged it and the blast hit Mo (who screamed). This made Rod laugh even harder.

Master Rackson had grown tired of this. "That's enough!" he said to his students. "Come here." The four of them walked towards the spectators, no doubt quite the sight. Rod was still wiping tears of laughter from his eyes, Mo's clothes were steaming from the combination of water and fire on them, M was still soaking wet, and De was clutching his chest.

"That was pathetic!" Master Rackson snapped. "You fought the others more than you fought your sparring partners!"

"He shouldn't of hit me," Rod protested, pointing at M. "Work on your aim before you get somebody killed!"

"Learn to get out of the way then!" M yelled in defense.

"ALL of you are to blame!" Master Rackson yelled over both of them. "I saw petty distractions, poor aiming, unnecessary attitudes and wasteful taunting, all things that could and would get you killed in a real battle!" Master Rackson's words hit home, as all four Elementals avoided his gaze in shame. Master Rackson sighed deeply. "Perhaps I was wrong. You four clearly need much more training in simply getting along with one another before you could have a prayer at taking over this factory, let alone facing A.G." Even Rose and Don were looking embarrassed now. "Go clean yourselves up; we're done for the day." He turned and walked back up the stairs.

Rose glanced after him and turned back to the students. "Don't worry; he's just a little on edge right now, he'll be fine after a while." She dashed upstairs to catch up with her brother, leaving Don and the Elementals alone in an uncomfortable silence.

"Ummm...I think it's about dinner time for me...Mo, if you wanna come by, just give me a call," and with that he also left the Elementals. Though none of them spoke, they all shared the same thought. If they didn't clean up their act soon, they would all be learning to work together in the factory.

Bonding in Black City

De was the last of the four to come out of the shower. Steam poured from the second floor bathroom as De walked outside of it still shirtless. He was a tad bit surprised to find the others all waiting for him in the hallway.

"I swear, you're *always* naked," M shook his head. De noticed a tad bit of jealousy in his tone.

De looked down at his brown chest and shrugged. "I'm comfortable like this. Why are you guys still here?" he asked. M and Rod lived in a town about 30 miles away, and Mo's house was on the other side of the city.

"The HNIC has an idea," Rod explained, his voice dripping with sarcasm.

M obviously didn't catch it. "Yes I do. Well, you know how Master Rackson said we have to learn to get along? Well, what better way for us to learn how to get along than for us to spend more time together?"

"I already don't like where this is going..." De muttered. His comments didn't faze M's excitement either.

"And since time is precious, I figured we should start ASAP! Soooo, I called my mom, and she said you could all come stay at my house tonight! That way we could spend the whole night and some of tomorrow training and just hanging together!" M finished, looking

quite proud of himself for thinking this up. His comrades, however, didn't look so enthusiastic. De's jaw dropped, and Rod dropped his head into his palm. Even Mo looked apprehensive.

"So, we would be staying at your house so we could hang out? All of us? In one place?" Mo asked.

M nodded profusely. "It'll be great! We can stay up talking and sparring and all kinds of stuff!"

"You're showing your age, kid," De pointed out. M's happiness started to fade when no one jumped at his suggestion.

"I'm in," Mo said after a moment. "It'll be the first time I've ever stayed with anyone else besides Don."

M began grinning anew, and turned to De. "I'm not gonna wake up to you standing over me with a knife, am I?" he asked. He wasn't so eager to place himself on the home turf of someone who hated him.

M suddenly became serious. "We may have our differences, but I am willing to put those aside for the sake of the team. Any good leader would do the same."

De opened his mouth to argue this, but decided against it. "If it's for the good of the team, and to take down A.G., I'll do it," All eyes turned to Rod. He looked back at the rest of them like he was the only sane person left.

"I already told you; my house is in Black City, why I gotta stay at yours?"

"And M already told you, it's a bonding exercise; it won't work unless we spend as much time as possible together," Mo said simply.

"I don't need to bond. I hate all you the same," He retorted.

"Oh come on man, it's only one night. What could happen?" De reasoned.

"Do you know what can happen in one night? My whole crew broke up in one night; I've robbed department stores blind in one night. A LOT can happen in one night."

"As your leader, I order you to come sleep at my house!" M barked.

Rod shook his head. "I'm gonna ignore how wrong that sounds," De snickered. "I respect that you've been with the Racksons the longest, but you not a leader. Even if you were, nothing is gonna get me to stay at your house," He said with finality.

M actually smiled at him. "I kinda thought you would say that. ROSE!" he yelled. Rose emerged from her bedroom down the hall from the bathroom. "He's not cooperating," M said to her, pointing at Rod.

Rose walked over to Rod to look him firmly in his eyes. He looked back at her with rebellion in his own. "What if I said that if you didn't do this I would tell your parole officer about your little rendezvous at the mall last week?"

Rod continued to stare at Rose. "I took everything back, you forget that part? You made me do it."

"But I'm pretty sure they won't be too happy that you stole those shoes from there in the first place. I think you all should take advantage of M's idea. Matty's right, you guys are going to have to learn to get along. If you can't learn to like each other as people, there is no way you're going to be able to fight together. And if you can't do that, A.G. and her android army are gonna tear you apart," she said.

Rod looked at Rose. When he saw she wasn't backing down, he did. "Fine...I'm in," was all he said. M smiled.

"Take my car. Mo can drive you all there and bring it and you back tomorrow," she tossed Mo her keys (which he dropped) and walked away.

"My house then?" M couldn't look any happier. "Trust me, this will be great for us!"

"What possessed me to bring you people here?! This is hopeless!" M screamed.

He, Mo, Rod and De had all paired off to spar after they had dinner at his home, but somehow the battles had gotten intertwined once again. It may have started when Rod used water from a nearby pond to put out some of De's flames, lost control of all the water and accidentally sent it everywhere. It may also have started when a few frogs came hopping out of the rushing pond water, and Mo (who was terrified of frogs) freaked out and started freezing everything around him, including his fellow Elementals who were covered in the pond water. However it started; it ended with everyone either freezing or soaked.

"You're the one that dragged us here!" Rod yelled over his shivering. "You said this junk would help us to like each other more, and guess what? I hate all of you even more now!"

"Just stop you guys!" De stepped in between M and Rod to stop any further violence between them. "Look, it's obvious that sparring isn't the kind of bonding we need. Besides, it's getting dark, and I can see some fog coming in,"

"Frogs? Where?" Mo yelled suddenly, glancing over his shoulders. That was enough to make everyone laugh at his fear. Mo, however, was not amused.

"You guys are mean...Don never treats me like this," he muttered.

"Well not everyone is like your little lackey friend. Some of us live in reality, not a cartoon," Rod shrugged. He took off the orange skull cap he had gotten from his house and wrung the water out of it.

Mo stared at Rod with the utmost dislike, prompting De to try to diffuse the tension. "Don't get upset Mo, we're just messing with you. You know we all cool. The only person we don't like is shorty here," De motioned to M, who was still trying to warm himself. He sneered at De's comment.

Mo sighed. "I'm sorry. I'm still getting used to...this..." he said, pointing around at all of them. He plopped down on the ground and didn't see the side eying Rod and M were giving him. De was once again playing peacemaker.

"I mean it's no problem. Your other friends don't rag on each other every once in a while?" De asked.

"I wouldn't know; don't have any," Mo said matter-of-factly. "Most folks kinda avoid me. Until Don came along, nobody wanted to hang with me, they all thought I was-um...lame."

"I wonder why..." Rod said sarcastically. He placed his hat back on his head and walked back to the pond to play in the water.

M squatted on the ground so he could look Mo in his eyes. "That's kind of sad, Mo. So you've only ever been friends with us and Don your whole life?" Mo nodded.

"Even I had some friends when I was at the shelter, you

can't shut yourself away from everyone else just because you don't think they'll like you," De said as he too, sat down with Mo.

"Shelter? Like, for abandoned kids? Are you an orphan?" Mo asked. He had never thought to ask about De's parentage.

De laughed. "Sort of. My parents got rid of me when I was little. Who knows why, maybe they weren't ready for a kid," De snapped his fingers and a small flame appeared at their tips. Mo jumped but kept listening. "I bounced around with some relatives for a while, but none of them could keep me for long. Next thing I know I'm in an orphanage. Nobody wanted to adopt the funny looking redhead kid, so I stayed there for about four years 'till I had an accident after a nightmare one night." De showed the flame on his fingers to the others to explain just what sort of accident he had.

"Did...did you hurt anyone?" Mo asked, scared of the answer.

"Nah. Room was burned pretty bad, but nobody got hurt. But I felt too guilty to stay there so I ran away. I lived on my own for a little while till this nice older couple took me in." De played around with the flame as he explained.

"What happened to them? Why don't you still live with them instead of with the Racksons?" M asked. Mo looked anxiously at De.

"Bad stuff tends to happen to people I'm around," De said simply. He waved his hand and the flame disappeared. "Let's just say I'm better off on my own, taking care of myself."

"Now there's something I can relate to," Rod said. He finally left the pond and took a seat on the ground with his comrades. "That's the story of my life man. What folks don't understand is that sometimes you gotta learn to do what it takes to provide for yourself and your folks." De nodded.

"Let me guess, this is the backstory of the Heat Boyz? Black City's most notorious group of thugs." M added for De and Mo's benefit.

"Call us what you want, but you know that we used to run this place. For a year me and my boy Jay had everyone in this town bolting down their doors as soon as the sun went down. We got some good stuff from it too," Rod said, reminiscing.

"How in the world did you end up here then?" De asked.

"The cops caught me and Jay one night. Some...some bad stuff happened and my boy got locked up. I got away, but only for a little while. Master Rackson worked out a deal with my parole officer, and I have a little more freedom than most so long as I keep coming to him at least three times a week. I think I would rather be on house arrest or something though...." Rod muttered.

"Oh come on, Rod. It can't be that bad being with us. Besides, if you were still on the path you were before you'd probably be working with A.G. right now," M shoved him playfully.

"That wouldn't be a bad idea....I'm kidding!" he added hastily, seeing the looks of horror on his teammates' faces. "I couldn't do that really; I couldn't be a killer." Rod stopped talking and stared off into space. There was a silence amongst the four for a minute.

M broke it. "Wow, I never knew you guys had such colorful histories. Guess that's why I have to be the leader of you psychos, since I'm the only normal one." He laid down on the ground so he couldn't see the dirty looks the other three were throwing his way.

"You talk like you don't have any issues, M," Mo said.

"I don't!" M said. "You guys know that my Dad is mayor of Black City since our family founded the city. Both of my parents are around and take care of me and my little brother, I do well in school and if my folks have anything to say about it I'll be in the best college around after I graduate with honors. My life is good," M explained. He continued to look up towards the setting sun and not at his comrades. Rod muttered not very quietly about how spoiled M was, but M didn't respond.

"Can we head back to your house now?" Mo asked after a moment.

"Sure. Maybe if I sleep on it I can come up with another way for us to get closer as a team," M yawned and led his friends back to his home.

The next morning the Elementals awoke to M's parents preparing them a hearty breakfast. They said goodbye to them and M's baby brother and drove to the woods on the outskirts of the city. M had the bright idea that spending the day together in nature would have no choice but to bring them closer. As they rode out of the city they passed the time by discussing how they would each take out A.G.

"I'd have the easiest time. All I would have to do is short circuit her! You guys distract her and open her up, I shoot a little shock in her circuits, and no more A.G.!" M boasted.

"Nobody but my Dad would know how to take A.G. apart, and you could shoot electricity at her body all day long, and it wouldn't do anything. She's made from a different metal than the other androids, you can't shock through it," Mo pointed out. He turned a corner onto a road near the woods.

"Oh..." M said, disappointed.

"Well is she rust proof? Get me a bunch of water and I'll have her creaking like an old joint," Rod suggested.

Mo shook his head. "Do you know how long it takes for metal to rust? You'll have to shoot water at her until you're thirty before she rusts. Especially considering what she's made of," Mo said.

"Ok Mr. Negative, how bout I just keep making hotter and hotter fire and keep shooting it at her? I bet her metal won't make it through *that*," De said proudly.

"Unless you can create a supernova and find a way to not kill everyone in the country, you can't do that either," Mo said grimly. "I'm sorry guys, but A.G.is just too powerful. Our only chance is to free my Dad, and hope that he can deactivate her someway."

"I see why no one wanted to hang with you, you're depressing," Rod muttered.

"I don't know, Mo. Master Rackson thinks we got a chance, so maybe he knows something about A.G. that we don't-" De began, but stopped suddenly when M grabbed his arm and pointed. "What? What is it?" he asked, looking where he was pointing.

"It's an android! They've come to Black City already!" he yelled. Sure enough, off the road and a few feet away from them on the other side of a small creek stood a metallic looking figure
among the trees. It appeared to be checking out the area around it; scoping it out for some reason.

"I've never seen an android wear cargos and a bandanna, or have locs..." Rod pointed out, looking at the supposed android's attire.

"Who cares! This is obviously one of A.G.'s henchmen, in *my* hometown! We have to take him out! Park the car, we gotta go fight him! Let's go team!" M said.

"Sounds like a plan...let's go for it!" De agreed. The two of them hopped out of the still moving car and took off towards the silver colored figure.

"This is gonna be trouble..." Rod shook his head, but leapt out and ran after the others anyway.

"Wait on me!" Mo yelled. He put the car in park by a nearby tree and followed after his comrades.

By the time Mo and Rod caught up with the other two, the "android" was already talking to De. As he spoke, it became obvious that he was not an android, but some strange silver-skinned man. He moved his black dreadlocks out of his face as he looked around at the four Elementals.

"You know, it's rude to just run up to someone and stare at them. What's the matter, never seen a silver guy before?" the Silver Man asked.

"What are you doing here? We already know that you work for A.G., so tell us why you are in Black City!" M snapped.

"You might wanna talk fast, before we're forced to hurt you." De threatened. He stepped forward and formed a flame in his hand to drive his point home.

The Silver Man eyed De with interest. "You people sure are brave. If you know what you claim you do and you still try to threaten me, you must think you have what it takes to take on Queen A.G.?"

"We're gonna take down you and that overgrown toaster you worship," Rod spat.

"Yeah, don't you know who we are? We're the

Elementals!" Mo piped in.

The Silver Man looked quite intrigued. "Really? Elementals, huh? Well Elementals, I'm afraid that I can't let you go running around with the knowledge you have, I'm gonna have to kill you now."

The second he finished speaking, the Silver Man stretched out his arms and pushed De backwards into the other three. The strange thing was, De was a full two feet away from the Silver Man. Obviously, the villain had the ability to stretch his limbs to unnatural lengths. The four barely had a chance to react to this development before his arms stretched towards them again. M raised his hands and shot two bolts of electricity at both of the Silver Man's arms, making him retract the silver colored limbs. Rod sent water from the creek rushing at the Silver Man, and Mo, in a fit of brilliance, froze the still rushing water on the Silver Man's body, trapping him in a layer of ice.

"Well would you look at that, you finally did something useful!" Rod praised him. Mo's triumph didn't last long however; the distinctive sound of a chainsaw was heard from within the Silver Man's ice prison. He had somehow transformed one of his hands into a chainsaw blade, and was busy chopping away at the ice that held him.

"What *is* this guy?!" Rod asked in alarm.

"I don't know, but he's gotta go!" De closed his eyes in focus, raised his hands and opened his eyes and sent a more continuous blast of fire in the Silver Man's direction. The roaring flames melted the ice around the Silver Man and the heat brought him to his knees. M aided De by firing off a few bolts of electricity; a particularly strong one caught the Silver Man in his chest and sent him flying backwards, deeper into the woods, with the Elementals in pursuit.

"Where is he?" Mo asked. All four of them searched the woods around them to try to find their adversary. The Silver Man dropped from a treetop and, this time forming his hands into hammers, tried to drop down onto De's head. Thankfully Rod was still close enough to the creek to bring water from it towards the Silver Man in midair, sending him careening into a tree and to the ground. Just as he did with Mo in their sparring session the previous day, Rod recycled the water to create a torrential jet of water on the Silver Man. The Silver Man reformed his left arm into a shield to try and block some of the water, leading M and De to add to Rod's attack with a few of their own. The Silver Man made the shield a little larger to compensate for the many attacks, but was brought to his knees once again by the Elementals. The villain formed a boomerang from his right hand, and threw it towards his attackers. The weapon struck De across the head, and ended his attack.

The Silver Man approached Rod with his shield still blocking most of the water, and stretched his other hand to grab him by his braids. He slung Rod away with his spare hand, stopping his attack as well.

With De's fires temporarily stopped Mo took this opportunity to freeze some of Rod's water into ice shards. When the Silver Man turned around to come after Mo the Ice Elemental sent enough shards of ice to pierce the Silver Man's shield and give M an opportunity to hit him full on with an electric bolt. The bolt electrocuted the Silver Man and he fell face forward to the ground.

"Is he dead?" Mo asked when the Silver Man didn't move for a moment.

"How are we supposed to know? Why don't you go check him?" M suggested.

"No way! Rod should go," Mo replied.

"So he can smack me with a hammer if he's still alive? I saw what he almost did to De, ain't no way," Rod protested.

"Fine, I'll check," De volunteered. With the other three creeping up behind him, De approached the motionless Silver Man. De reached his hand out to the silver neck to check for a pulse, and the Silver Man sprung back to life. De leapt backwards, and the Silver Man extended his arm and swung another hammer-shaped weapon at the Elementals. The four of them ducked, giving the Silver Man the time he needed. He retracted his arm and raced out of the woods.

"After him!" M yelled. The Elementals chased after the Silver Man, but when they got close he turned around and swung what seemed to be a spike-less mace at them. The ball and chain missed M and Mo, but caught Rod across the chest and De's side, bringing the two of them to an unsteady halt. M and Mo went to check on their comrades, but by the time they were certain De and Rod were fine and they caught up with the Silver Man he was sitting in Rose's car, right where Mo had left it.

"Please tell me you didn't leave the keys in the car…" De whispered.

"I was excited, everybody was running off to go fight and I forgot," Mo whispered back. De shook his head sadly as the Silver Man had started the car and grinned at the Elementals.

"Maybe you are a little stronger than I thought, but you're a lot dumber. Thanks for the ride!" He laughed and drove off into the distance with the Elementals' only mode of transportation. M tried to fire off another bolt of electricity, but it missed both the car and the Silver Man, and he was gone.

"Man...Rose is gonna kill us..." was all Rod could say.

To the Center

The four Elementals walked back to M's house and cleaned themselves up after their battle with the mysterious Silver Man. Without transportation it would be very hard for them to get Mo and De back home, let alone get to Rackson Manor for training that day, so they called the Racksons to tell them what happened.

"...and you say he could change shape?" Master Rackson asked over the phone. Rose continued complaining about her car in the background.

"Yeah, he turned his hands into a hammer, a shield and some more stuff. He even stretched his arms out like stupid long," De explained.

Master Rackson was silent on the other end for a moment. "I think you four need to get here. Judging by recent events it's obvious that A.G. is going to great lengths to bring about total control as quickly as possible. We cannot waste any more time."

"Ummm, how?" De asked.

"What did he say?" M questioned, but De shushed him so he could hear Master Rackson's answer.

"...Alright Master Rackson. We'll be there as soon as we can," De said, and hung up the phone. He turned to give his comrades the unpleasant news that Master Rackson wanted them to get back to Rumas. Immediately, which meant they may have to walk.

"Is he NUTS?" Rod asked.

"We'll die before we get there! We can't walk 30 miles!" Mo complained.

"He said that his generation of Elementals walked all over Sylver Continent in their day. But he said we could stop in Center City and he'll have somebody there bring us the rest of the way," De continued.

"That's still about ten miles. And it's still early morning, which means we may be walking in the heat of the day," M said.

"Well it's either go or not go. Master Rackson made it seem pretty important that we get there ASAP," De said. The others took a moment to weigh the option of disappointing their instructor and being lazy.

"You did say that spending the day together in nature is just what we need...this is about as natural as you get," Mo reasoned.

M sighed. "Fine...I guess since Mom and Dad are stuck at work until tonight we will have to walk. Let's go, team," he said reluctantly.

"Man..." Rod wiped sweat from his forehead as he spoke. The foursome had been walking for about eight miles already. "I thought good guys got perks? Why can't we get a car or some kinda ride back?"

"Because the good guys aren't that popular right now,"

De said.

"Just give me the word, guys, and I'll get us a car like that," Rod offered, snapping his fingers for emphasis.

"No way, dude, there are enough criminals out here already, we don't need to add ourselves," De said with a sigh.

"Besides," M heaved. He had to stay behind and make sure Mo kept up. He had spent a lot of the past five miles shoving him forward. Even now, Mo tripped over a rock on the side of the road and M, small as he was, had to help him up. "You of all people should know that breaking into cars will only lead to trouble. Isn't that how you ended up with us in the first place?"

Rod shrugged, unconcerned. "Why do...why do you say that?" Mo breathed in M's ear. M shoved him off his shoulders and stepped back to address the group. "Didn't you guys know? That's how Rod got to meet Master Rackson in the first place! Rod broke into his car, thinking it was a teacher's, and completely flooded the inside of it. Cost Master Rackson a pretty penny from what Rose was saying one day..." All eyes turned to Rod, who actually laughed. M did not look pleased that his story had no negative effect on him.

"Yea, it did. But the old man told me if I came and cleaned his floors for him I could get away with it," Rod walked in front of De and turned around so that he could address all three of them at once.

"So there I was, thinking that this has got to be the stupidest guy alive, and he turned out to be smarter than I thought. He knew that I would use my powers to clean up and get out of there, so when he caught me he gave me two options: Either stay there and learn to use my powers 'for good', or really get charged for the damages," Rod laughed again. "Guess which one I chose?"

De and M chuckled, but Mo looked thoughtful. "Well that was good that Master Rackson helped you," he said.

"What do you mean? I wasn't in trouble; I don't need his help," Rod asked, walking a little closer to him.

Mo backed up a little bit. Rod was only slightly taller than him but his muscle tone made him look largely intimidating to the frailer Elemental. "I just mean it was good he gave you a positive outlet...I mean, you could've ended up in real trouble; like that Jay kid you used to hang with. You're better than that."

"So you just know everything about me huh? You remember the name of my best friend and just think you're an expert on me and my life? You don't know anything about me and what I've been through or what I've done. The Racksons didn't just wave a magic wand and fix my life, this ain't no fairy tale, kid,"

De grabbed Rod's shoulder and pulled him away. "Leave him alone, man. He doesn't know any better," Rod shrugged De off and kept walking ahead. Mo wanted to remind them that he very likely knew more than them, but thought against it. They soon passed a sign that informed them that Center City was only 1.5 miles away.

"Thinking about Rod's story makes me wonder," M said out loud. Rod groaned. "How did *you* meet the Racksons, De?" he asked.

De said nothing, but M pressed on. "I mean, my parents always knew I was gonna be great. When the blood tests came back to say I was an Elemental they started sending me to the Racksons when I was 12, just in case I developed my powers early. And Mo's dad is good friends with them, so he knew where to go when his powers developed. But what about you...?"

"It's not important," De said simply. Mo nudged M, trying to convince him to drop the subject, but M wouldn't give up that easily.

"Sure it is! We heard Rod's riveting tale, so why not yours? It's not like we'll be getting there too soon; we need some entertainment."

"I don't want to talk about it," De started to walk a little faster away from them.

"Just tell him the story; he won't shut up until you do," Rod commented. His tone of voice suggested that he too, was a little curious as to their newest comrade's origins. He had, after all, only been with the team for a couple weeks.

"No," De kept his focus on the road ahead of them; trying desperately to keep his voice from rising. M continued to mutter behind him until it was Mo, not De, who had had enough.

"He doesn't want to tell you guys because he met them after he tried to kill me," He said finally.

De, M, and Rod all stopped immediately. De kept facing forward, obviously too ashamed to show his face. M and Rod kept looking from De to Mo with their mouths wide open in shock.

"Wait, what?" M stuttered.

"Wow..." Rod said.

Mo bit his lip nervously. He had changed the entire mood of the walk and he didn't like it. He looked at his feet as he continued. "I mean, he had a good reason..." Rod opened his mouth to say something sarcastic but M touched him and shook his head to shut him up.

"No, I didn't," De said, still facing forward. "I was going to…hurt Mo by association, and it was completely unfair," he sighed and turned to look at the others. "You remember the old couple I told you guys that took me in? Well, they didn't just die…they were killed by some androids."

Understanding washed over Rod, but poor M was still lost. "And then what?" he asked like the eager child he was.

"He did his research," Mo said to his shoes. De shook his head sadly and turned around at last.

"He found out that my Dad created A.G. and tracked us down. While Dad and Lauryn were out one day he came to my house for revenge," Mo continued.

With M finally caught up (complete with a loud "Oh!"), De finished the story. "I was so mad…I wanted to take his whole family out and find a way to get A.G. too. She took away the only family I had ever had, and I wanted to make all of them pay. I was ready to um, finish the job when Prof. Peters and Rose walked in. It took Rose maybe twenty seconds to take me out and save Mo. When I came to I was in Rackson Manor getting drilled by Master Rackson."

He breathed heavily and turned back around and kept walking. Rod followed him. M, however, was still not satisfied. He hung back and whispered to Mo: "What happened then?"

Mo chuckled. "I limped in and told Master Rackson that he had a good reason for doing what he did. The stories matched up, and they decided that he would be a useful addition to the team."

M whistled. "Wow, I never knew. I wondered where he came from when he just popped up in training sessions one day but no one would ever say. I should've just asked you, huh?" M leaned in even closer to Mo to question him further. "Between me and you, you must still hold some sort of grudge, right? I mean, he almost killed you for something you had nothing to do with. Do you feel comfortable around him? Because if not..."

Mo stopped walking completely and backed away from M. "Not at all. De had every reason to seek revenge for what happened. If I was in his shoes I would've done the exact same thing. The fact that he did his research and found us shows how dedicated he is to taking down A.G., and I respect him for that."

M waved his hands in defense. "I'm sorry. I didn't mean to offend you. I just thought..." he took a deep breath. "I guess you're right though, he is kinda legit," he turned back fully forward and came face to chest with De himself. Rod shook his head behind De as M backed away, embarrassed.

"We're here." De said, pointing to another sign. This one read "Welcome to Center City.

Under Siege and Overwhelmed

"'One of the Great Lands most important locales: Center City is a farming community where over 100 farms grow the produce and raise the livestock our great country uses for nourishment.'" Mo read off a historical marker inside the city.

"We all know about Center City," Rod pointed out. "They put their labels on *everything*. 'Center City's finest milk, Center City's finest eggs, Center City's finest beef.' It's probably on the people, too. 'Center City's finest teacher, Center City's finest criminal,'" he laughed at himself.

M and De laughed too, but Mo looked confused. "How can a person be fine and a criminal?"

"Just laugh and move on, Mo," De patted him on the back as M and Rod laughed even harder. They looked around the few buildings in what seemed to be the town square. Predictably, Center City didn't bother much with building too many fancy structures, since they were so close to both Black City and Rumas. Just when they started to wonder where they would find the man that Master Rackson had set them up with a short and fit man with a brown skin tone sprinted towards the Elementals.

"Excuse me, would you young'ins happen to be them there...uh...Elementals?" his drawling voice made it hard for the Elementals to figure out his question, and his red shirt, dirty overalls, and boots covered in a substance that may or may not have been mud told them that he was a farmer.

"Ummm, yes...who are you?" Mo asked, looking at the squat little man.

"Dearest apologies y'all. My name is Oscar Torrac. Imma farmer here in Center City, and my ol' buddy Matt Rackson called and said that you guys would be coming up and to be looking for ya." Farmer Torrac took off his hat and bowed as he introduced himself, revealing the top of his balding head.

"Oh, ok Farmer Torrac. I'm De..." De began introducing them, before M interrupted.

"This is Rod, Mo, and I am M, the leader. Now, I have a few questions for you 'Farmer Torrac': How do we know that you are truly a friend? Seems kinda odd that somebody would be here just waiting on us to show up," M eyed the man; possibly because he was one of the few people M could look square in the eye.

Rod pushed M out of the way as Farmer Torrac struggled to think of an answer that would satisfy the raging Elemental. "Don't pay attention to him," De told the man.

"Well...okay..." he couldn't help but notice M looking suspiciously at him from under Rod's arm. "Well, at any rate, I'm so glad y'all got here safely. Things've been mighty rough 'round here, even for people with powers like y'alls. Come on by the house; me and Sharon'd love to have y'all over," He motioned for the Elementals to follow him to his car.

"What's wrong with you? Obviously this is the guy

Master Rackson had meet us," Rod asked M as soon as Farmer Torrac was out of earshot.

"How do we know that? He could be one of A.G.'s spies! I'm doing what any good leader would do, protecting my team from danger! But *you* wouldn't know anything about that, would you now?" M yelled.

"So that's the game you wanna play, huh?" Rod's voice rose to match M's as he pushed the Electric Elemental backwards. De quickly stepped in between the two again.

"Cut it out guys! Look, clearly this guy wants to help us, so we should go with him. Besides, if he is leading us to a trap, it's nothing the four of us can't get ourselves out of, right?" he asked.

"Right!" Mo said, trying to lighten the mood with way too much enthusiasm. Rod and M just stared at him, and M stormed off to follow Farmer Torrac to his car. Once M got in, Rod walked off as well and made sure he sat in the front, away from M. Mo stopped De before he could follow.

"Nobody else but Master Rackson has ever stopped Rod from fighting somebody," Mo pointed out.

"Oh, that was nothing...I used to have to break up kids fighting all the time at the orphanage," De admitted.

"No, it was pretty cool. Maybe you should be our leader instead of M. You are doing a better job at it already..." Farmer Torrac had gotten impatient and started blasting his horn at Mo and De, and the two had to rush to join the others.

"This is delicious, Mrs. Torrac!" De thanked his gracious hosts.

"This chicken is awesome!" M agreed.

"Good stuff," Rod added from the end of the table. Mo

contributed only smacking and a head nod to the exchange.

"I'm glad y'all like it," Mrs. Torrac beamed at the hungry teens. Her smile seemed to cover her whole face; from the roots of her short afro to her sharp chin. "It's been a while since we've had company; them androids ain't good for the travelling crowd."

Mo finally swallowed his food and spoke: "Yea, we had to take out like eight of them on the way here…."

"You mean *we* had to take out eight of them while you hid behind bushes," Rod pointed out, making M snicker into his drink. He realized what he did and pretended to be angry again.

"There's a whole lot of the devils hangin' 'round now," Farmer Torrac picked up, ignoring Mo's disgruntled expression. "On account of the siege and all."

"What siege?" Rod asked, suddenly getting serious.

"You mean to tell me y'all ain't heard? Well I reckon I shouldn't be too surprised, it's only been a day since they started it." Farmer Torrac admitted.

"Started what? What is going on?" M stared intently at Farmer Torrac, demanding answers.

"Sarah ain't you ready for bed?" Mrs. Torrac said suddenly. Despite the toddler's protests, she removed her from the high chair and carried her out of the room. Once they heard Sharon's footsteps hit the top of the stairs Farmer Torrac leaned forward and began his story.

"Well, yesterday A.G.'s hoodlums heard tell of a resistance in Rumas. Some folks were talking 'bout going to the factory she's buildin' there and shuttin' it down before it even gets up good. Well, she couldn't have that, so she sent some of those metal contraptions to lock up the whole city until she could fish them out. So right 'bout now Rumas is dead; nobody can get in or out and she's sending in extras to keep it that way." Farmer Torrac sat back in his seat to let this new info sink in right when his wife returned.

The Elementals were silent for a minute. The only sounds heard were the muffled cries of the Torracs' young daughter trying to avoid sleep upstairs. At last it was M who spoke.

"So, everyone in Rumas is under siege...because of us," the guilt in his voice was reflected in the other three's faces.

"Now hold on now, nobody said it was y'all fault! These resistance folks could be anybody; if it's even real. We all hate that thing for messin' up our lives! Heck, if I could I'd start up a 'resistance' myself. Do you know how much she's stolen from us to feed them people she keeps locked up in them factories?" Mrs. Torrac ranted.

"That's nice of you, Mrs. Torrac, but we all know it's us she's after. Nobody else would be brave or stupid enough to say anything bad about her," M said matter-of-factly.

"I think you underestimatin' normal people, son. You start messin' with folks' happiness, separatin' families, terrorizin' homes and takin' away freedoms and they'll do some crazy things," Farmer Torrac declared. M still looked unconvinced.

"Regardless of who the resistance is, A.G. heard about it and reacted, now we have to react too. I think we need to go now, guys," De said.

Rod and Mo nodded, but M was livid. "When did I die and make you leader?!" He demanded, getting up from the table to glare at De.

"He is doing a pretty good job of it..." Mo said quietly; avoiding M turning to stare at him.

Rod was of course, unfazed by M's attitude. "I agree with De. A.G. is holding the city hostage and we have to do something."

M rolled his eyes in Rod's direction but took his seat. Despite his desire to be in charge at all times, he knew a good idea when he heard one, even if it came from his rival.

"I like y'all enthusiasm, but y'all shouldn't go tonight." Mrs. Torrac suggested.

"But Master Rackson wanted us to get to Rumas as soon as we could," De pointed out.

"I'll give Matt a holler; y'all shouldn't bother tryna go to town until tomorrow, I doubt they'll even let you through. 'Sides, If you're gonna go retake Rumas at least do it after a good night's sleep." Farmer Torrac offered.

"Good idea! Team, we'll do that!" M said quickly before anyone else could respond. Even Mo rolled his eyes at M's audacity.

"That'll be fine. Sharon and I'll make up our guest room." Farmer Torrac said, getting up from the table.

About thirty minutes later once everything was cleaned up and the Torracs were all gone to bed, the four Elementals walked into the guest room, and immediately three of them ran and jumped on the bed to try to claim it. De, M, and Mo became a tangled mess of limbs and competiveness when they all landed together.

"I need the bed! I'm the leader!" M said.

"I'm the oldest!" Mo complained.

"I need it; I can't scrunch up in that chair!" De protested.

Rod shook his head as his teammates continued to

argue over who would sleep in the bed. "Can you guys shut up for a second?" he finally said.

"Can't you see we're trying to settle something here?" M said. He turned to Rod. "Somebody's gotta sleep in the bed. How else do you suppose we do to decide?"

"I don't care, you guys can fight over it if you want, just shut up about it," Rod grabbed a set of sheets that Mrs. Torrac had given them out of the chair in the corner of the room and started to make himself a pallet on the floor.

The three Elementals who still wanted the opportunity to sleep in the bed started to wonder how they would decide. "Well, two of us could sleep up here," De suggested, looking at the size of the bed.

"And one of them should be me!" M said loudly, and the arguing started again. Rod rolled his eyes and put his stocking cap on his braids. Luckily it was still in his pocket when their car got stolen.

"I have an idea!" Mo said after a minute. "We could have a contest, like a staring contest or something to figure out which two get to sleep in the bed!"

M, De, and even Rod stared at Mo for a moment.

"What? It was an idea," Mo said shamefully.

"I have a better one, come here M," Rod said. When the shortest Elemental approached Rod, he grabbed his afro and yanked a hair out of it.

"Ow! What was that about?" M demanded, rubbing his head.

"I'm solving the problem. Come here you two, pull a hair. The longest two hairs can sleep in the bed. The shortest one can sleep on the chair here," Rod said.

When the other two walked towards M he quickly

raised his hands to stop them. "That's ok! That's ok! You two can have the bed!"

"I figured as much. You're welcome," Rod laughed and bowed to De and Mo before settling on the floor. M mumbled to himself but grabbed a blanket and a pillow and curled up in the chair. Thankfully, his size made this fairly easy.

"You criminal mastermind," De chuckled. He sat down on one end of the bed, as Mo and the others tried to get as comfortable as their Skin Armor clothes would allow (their normal clothes were still in the car that the Silver Man stole) and laid where they would be sleeping.

"Nah, if I was a mastermind I wouldn't have gotten caught," Rod pointed out. "I'm just a simple ex-gang leader."

"You would've gotten caught eventually though," Mo said.

Instead of getting angry, Rod just laughed. "You are gonna have to learn that real life isn't like those TV shows you and your boyfriend watch, sometimes the 'bad guys' be okay."

"Don's not my boyfriend!" Mo protested loudly. Even in the room's dim light, De could tell that the Elemental in the bed with him had turned red. Only he seemed to notice Mo's discomfort at the suggestion.

De decided to change the subject. "Hey Rod, what do you plan on doing once we beat A.G.?"

"Me? Well once we take her out I'm going back to my regular life," Rod said.

"So does that mean terrorizing Black City? Stealing and selling that stuff?" M reached up to turn off the light and ran and fell back into his chair.

Rod shrugged. "Maybe. It's what I know," He looked at the others in the room expecting some sort of reaction, but no one said anything. He sighed. "You know, you guys could play along. Act like you care that I might end up in jail."

"That would be on you if you did," De said. He kicked off his shoes and laid on the bed so that he and Mo were head to foot, with De's head near the headboard. Mo moved over to make room for De's long legs and De continued. "You gotta not wanna go to jail to stay out of it."

"I don't *want* to go to jail, nobody *wants* to go to jail, they just end up there," Rod said.

"Well why do you think you will end up there?" M asked.

"You know how you have both of your parents working day in and day out to take care of you and your little brother?" Rod asked. When M nodded he continued. "Well I don't. Ma works hard by herself to try to take care of me and Jas. Jas is my little sister," he added when De looked confused.

"So is that why you started up the Heat Boyz? To make things easier for your mom?" De asked, but Rod said nothing.

Mo finally spoke again. "That's why my Dad created Lauryn. He got kinda lonely so he made her some years after my Mom died.

"When did your mom die?" M asked.

"When I was really little; like five. I just remember my dad being really sad for a really long time," Mo rolled towards the wall and continued speaking towards it. "I remember being sad a lot too, but I stopped being depressed when I met Don. He made Lauryn after that and we finally got stuff back on track. After we get my Dad back all of us can go back to our normal lives again."

"You and them are really close, huh?" De asked. Mo nodded and rolled over to look at him, but De asked no other questions.

M still had something to say. "Well, I plan on staying leader and helping the Racksons find the other Elementals in our generation. It's supposed to be ten of us, you know."

"Yea we all had Elemental history lessons," Rod said. "Technically it's nine of us now, since, you know…"

"What?" De and Mo said at the same time.

"Master Rackson's son died. He was a Morph Elemental that Master Rackson said got killed by A.G.," M said simply. The room got quiet for a moment, as they all no doubt were overcome by the same worry. It was Rod who broke the silence.

"What about you, De? What are you gone do after we take out the head honcho?"

"I don't know. I don't really have a home to go to. I guess I could stick around for a little while, and see how this Elemental thing plays out. Who knows, maybe I'll get some fans after we save the world and I can go live with one of them!" De stretched out on the bed and his feet popped out from under the sheets. He laughed at himself in spite of the sad realization he came to. Everyone got quiet again as they all started to get sleepy.

Mo had one last comment. "M? Did you really want to sleep in the bed?"

M poked his head out from under his blanket. "Nah, I'm comfortable now; don't wanna move. Why?"

"Because…De's feet are making me lightheaded…" Mo replied.

"Hey! They're not that bad…" De argued, but nonetheless moved them away from Mo's head. M and Rod laughed out loud, and Mo, noticing that he had made a joke, laughed too. Even De had to join in eventually.

"You people are crazy…" Mo closed his eyes and allowed himself to drift off to sleep.

Early the following morning, the Elementals awoke to find Farmer Torrac already up and waiting on them. He offered to drive them as close to the city as he could get so they could save their energy for getting inside the city. They ended up a little less than a mile outside of the city before he was forced to turn around.

"This is 'bout as far as I can go. Y'all will have to go the rest of the way yallselves. Good luck Elementals, I'm rooting for y'all!" he called as he drove off.

"Big chicken. He saw all the androids and hauled it outta here. All that junk about resisting and he couldn't even take us into the city," complained Rod.

"Well, he doesn't have any powers to defend himself, so can you blame him?" De asked. Rod shrugged and they started walking into the city limits. The moment they got in range of the androids patrolling them the battle was on.

They fought through a dozen of A.G.'s mechanical henchmen before they climbed to the top of a mountain overlooking Rumas. The many androids they fought and the fact that the actual roads were blocked off kept them from using the main roads to get into the city, and they had to follow a shortcut through the woods outside the city. This small mountain was the last bit of nature before they reached the urban area of the city, and it gave them the opportunity to get a full view of just how closed off Rumas was.

The four heroes breathed heavily as they glanced past

the waterfall to the city streets. It was still fairly busy for a weekend morning, but it was also very full of androids.

"Those guys are freaking everywhere!" Mo complained. "Are we sure we can do this?"

"Of course we can! We have to," M breathed.

Rod bent over to get a better look. "I think they spotted us!" And sure enough, they were soon peppered with laser fire as about six androids noticed the four teens who didn't belong on the hill.

"Halt! Trespassing civilians, you have been cornered!" the four turned around to see that at least six more androids had snuck up behind them. The heroes backed into each other; trying to weigh their options.

Rod grabbed M as the androids closed in on them. "Well, you wanna be our leader so bad, lead!"

Words seemed to fail M at that moment. "Ummm...I...We..." he stammered.

"Think of something!" Mo was beginning to panic.

De shot a glance down the mountain. Those androids were still a few feet away from the lake at the bottom of it. They might have a shot...

"Follow me!" he called, and the Fire Elemental started running down the side of the hill. The six androids on the hill began firing their lasers, forcing the others to follow him. De started pitching flames at the oncoming androids, managing to slow some of them down.

"Help me out, Mo!" Rod yelled. He tossed his hand towards the nearby waterfall and sent a wave under the four of them which rushed away from the side of the mountain and into the air. Mo understood quickly and froze the wave as they went sliding down the ice ramp that launched the four of them over the androids on the ground. Predictably, the androids that were atop the mountain had followed them, so De threw more fire at the ice ramp, melting it and causing their enemies to collapse on each other in a big android pile up.

M started shooting bursts of electricity at the androids, but he was too exhausted to do any real damage to over a dozen of the creations. Mo tried throwing the remaining shards of ice at the androids, but with no luck.

"I can't hurt them!" he cried out, running backwards from the onslaught.

"Then get out the way!" Rod barked. He looked towards the small lake and started sending water towards the androids.

By now, the androids were firing their laser attacks at the Elementals, forcing them to try and dodge them in addition to attacking themselves. However, their exhaustion from having fought so many of A.G.'s forces already was showing: attacks that should have at least blasted the metal menaces backwards were bouncing off their exteriors.

"Guys, we gotta run!" Mo yelled. He went running sideways away from the battle deeper into the city.

"No way I'm losing to these can openers!" Rod snapped, still trying to stop the onslaught and avoid getting blasted by lasers.

In the distance, Mo screamed. M stopped trying to electrocute androids long enough to see his comrade being dragged by one of the "female" androids with her "hair" pulled back in a tight ponytail. She was flanked by six more of the machines, all of which raised their weapons to join in the fray.

"No!" M yelled. He ran towards the new group of androids to try and save Mo, only to be caught by at least four of the androids' blasts. The force of the blasts knocked him on his back, clothes singed and unconscious.

"I don't like how this is looking, De!" Rod admitted. He had given up trying to stop the androids and instead had ducked down behind the remains of a home the androids had destroyed prior.

"We can't give up! We have to-ugh!" halfway through De's pep talk he leaned from behind the building remains and got hit with a laser blast in the chest. He crumpled into a heap, leaving Rod alone.

"No!" Rod exclaimed. He shook De, trying to wake him, but he was out cold. Rod looked up to face down the two dozen of the androids.

"The resistance has been quelled, prepare for imprisonment, Elemental civilian," The androids chanted in a canopy of voices. Desperate and unwilling to go down without a fight, Rod pulled the gun from his pocket and fired off a few shots. The bullets hit maybe two androids, but did no damage. However, the laser attacks they responded with did do damage, and Rod fell.

The Underground Prison

Mo woke up with a start. He looked around frantically before realizing he wasn't facing down twenty plus androids anymore.

"Well, the nerd's up," Rod said bitterly.

"Funny how he's the first knocked out but the last to wake up," M remarked.

"Guys? Where are we?" Mo asked. He struggled to get up from the floor he was laying on and realized it was due to his hands being tied behind his back. He finally managed and looked around at where he was. His mouth gaped open, and he walked to the bars of what was unmistakably a jail cell. He peeked between the bars and saw Rod in a cell across from him.

"We're in jail," Rod shook his head. "For a smart guy, you're pretty stupid." It seemed that the four of them had been stuffed into cells in this small cell block. Mo was the only one on his side of the hallway, and there was only a single door far to the right of him.

"Leave Mo alone, Rod," De called. "Besides, we need to find a way out of here..." His cell was the farthest from the other three; on the same side as M and Rod and separated by three other cells so he could barely see the others.

"You've been suggesting that for ten minutes straight, and we've always come up with the same answer: we're stuck. We can't move our hands to use our powers and no one is around that's gonna let us out," M scoffed.

"As much as I hate to say it...M is right. Might as well accept it," Rod sat down on the cold floor of his cell and said, surprisingly quietly, "Never thought I'd be in jail for doing the *right* thing," De started to protest this once again when a light appeared at the end of the row of cells.

"Civilian Resistance leader: you and your cohort have been foolish to oppose Queen A.G., and because of your foolishness you will be imprisoned," An android explained as it shoved someone in the cell next to De.

"You guys are foolish! I know all of your schematics, you know!" this voice seemed familiar to the Elementals, even though none of them could see him for the two androids. M, Rod and Mo all looked at each other trying to figure out who it could be.

"If I ever get out of here I could disassemble you faster than you could turn around! Let me go!" the angry threats, however, fell on deaf ears. The android closed the cell and left. Mo heard the man shuffle around in the cell before it registered in him whose voice it was.

"Wait, is that...Don?!"

The Elementals' ally leapt from his bed and ran to try and get a view of his best friend. "Oh no! They caught you guys too!" he said, seeing the others in their cells.

"Don, what are you doing here?
Why'd they capture you?" De tried to angle himself so he could see some part of Don from his cell.

"Isn't it obvious? I'm part of the resistance! At least, I was until they caught us," Don replied. "They stormed the house a few hours ago and caught us all."

"'Us all'? Don what is going on?" M asked.

"You guys haven't heard? It was about twenty of us! A bunch of people just got sick of it all, so they banded together and decided that it was time for A.G. and her henchmen to go! I mean, how could we let one android dictate the rest of our lives? It seemed like a good idea at the time, that is until we actually got together and we realized that only Lauryn and I had any idea what to really do..."

"Lauryn?! She's in the resistance?" Mo interrupted.

"In it?" Don laughed. "She practically is-er, was the resistance. After your Dad got sent to jail, she called me and said she was sick of doing nothing. She said that she was gonna prove that Prof. Peters' creations were not inherently evil. She wanted to chase the androids out of Rumas so she could prove that."

"She has guts, that's for sure," Rod commented.

"Well, I thought she *didn't* have brains when she first told me about it. Then, she explained that the Professor had stowed away a bunch of self-defense weapons from when he used to fight with Mr. Rackson and Ms. Rose!" Don continued.

"That makes sense. Dad always told me that if anybody ever came to the house that wasn't supposed to be there to get to the lab to fight them off," Mo remembered. "Keep going, Don."

"Lauryn said she needed me to figure out how to work

the weapons, like I wouldn't have begged to do it anyway! I mean authentic Generation Immortal weapons! It was just like on *Brawling Bots* when they found the time capsule full of stuff from back when..."

"Don, please focus...what happened after Lauryn asked you to help with the weapons?" De pleaded over Rod's muttering of "I'm surrounded by idiots and cartoon freaks."

"Yeah, sorry. I said sure, and she called up some other people she had been talking to, and we all met up at your house," he looked towards Mo and continued. "That was when Lauryn told us her plan. I brought out all the weapons and just about everybody was on board! We were going to storm the factory and take it over, it was perfect!"

"Guess dung boots was right, normal people can do some crazy things," M admitted. "But if your plan was so perfect, what went wrong?"

Don's smile faltered a little. "Well, what we didn't find out until later was that the police had bugged Mo's house, I guess trying to frame Prof. Peters even further..."

"Oh no..." Mo said

"Police are good for stuff like that," Rod reminded him. "So lemme guess, the androids intercepted or overheard the messages?" The Elementals had learned that A.G.'s forces used police stations and their surveillance equipment to quell any possible uprisings. Letting police know that you were planning something was a surefire way to let the androids know the same.

"I'm thinking intercepted, but yea, they did. Early the next morning A.G. came on TV and said that Rumas was on lockdown because of the resistance. Lauryn and I tried to tell people that she couldn't possibly know who we all were, but a lot of people were still scared off by it. We had another meeting and decided to move the attack up to today, to get it over with before we lost anybody else," Don continued.

"...And the androids were there waiting on you," De finished, and Don nodded, his smile was completely gone now.

"I-it wasn't pretty. The androids were everywhere; all over the city, all over the factory. We didn't stand a chance. I don't even know how many of us survived..."

"That must be why we saw so many androids in the city today...they were all waiting on something to happen," M guessed.

Mo, however, wasn't focused on the number of androids in the city: he was only focused on one. "Don...where is Lauryn?"

Don looked back at Mo sadly. "...I don't know. It was so crazy; we just got separated and I don't know what happened to her. I'm so sorry, Mo."

Mo slumped back down to the floor of his cell and said nothing more.

M looked towards his comrade's cell "I'm sure she made it, Mo. I mean, she's made from the same stuff that they are, so she's gotta be just as tough."

De joined in. "Yea, she's probably on the run, waiting for the resistance to pick back up," De then addressed Don, "You didn't mention the Racksons anywhere in that story, didn't you guys get their help?"

"No," Don shook his head. "Lauryn was confident in her plan, but she didn't want to bring any Elementals down with us if something went wrong."

"That was smart of her. Too bad we went down anyway. We're stuck in here, just like you are," Rod turned away from the bars of his cell and sat on the bed inside of it.

"Can't you use your powers to get us out?" Don asked.

"No. We can't use them because our hands are tied," M explained. He turned so that Don could see his bound hands.

"You can't use them any other way? I mean, in the show *Storm Kings* they can channel their powers from just about any limb..." Don began.

"Too bad this is real life and not that show, then," Rod snapped.

Don, however, was not discouraged. "De, didn't you kick up some fire at M when you guys were fighting at the Manor the day before yesterday?"

De squinted as he tried to remember. "You know what, I think I did...I'm sure it must have been an accident though, like some kind of gut reaction to M trying to electrocute me..."

"Trying?" M interjected, but De and Don ignored him.

"Well, see if you can't react to being locked in here and kick up some more fire!" Don encouraged.

"Come on De, you can do it," Mo said, as M and Rod looked on with interest. De looked down at his feet and breathed deeply. It was going to be up to him to get them free. He closed his eyes and focused just like Master Rackson had told him so many times before. He kicked at the rusty iron bars with all of his might-and connected his foot with the bars.

"OUCH!!!" he screamed, falling down in agony. M began to laugh loudly.

"Well, we're screwed." Rod said. De apologized in between grunts of pain.

"It's ok De at least you tried," Don said.

"So what else can we do?" Mo asked. The rest of his friends shrugged.

De lifted himself to his feet. He stumbled again and leaned against the bars of his cell for support, and released a heavy sigh. Almost instantly he felt a rush of warmth reach over the bars. Confused, he exhaled again, deeper this time, and a tiny ember hit the bars.

"Guys...I think I can get us out of here after all!"

Everyone who could scrambled to get a look at De in his cell. De took as deep a breath as he could muster and exhaled pure flame unto the corner of the bars. The old bars creaked and burned hotter and hotter under the unfiltered heat of De's flaming breath, allowing him to kick the door off the hinges after a few moments.

"Wait, how did you do that?" Mo asked.

M answered. "It makes sense. One of the things that separate the Elementals from others with powers is the fact that our powers will grow and we'll learn new abilities."

"I'm guessing you ended up missing that one on the test I helped you study for," Don grinned at Mo. He turned to De and smiled even wider. "Well, I think this is the first time I've been happy to be around someone with really hot breath!" Don exclaimed, his smile back in full force.

M rolled his eyes. "Ugh...De, get me out first so I can strangle him..."

After De was able to free everyone from their cells and their handcuffs (they were just as old and rusty as the bars), it was time for them to figure out where they were. "I know they took me into some deep tunnel after they caught me, so if I had to guess I would say that we are somewhere in the Underground Kingdom," Don figured.

The others looked around the hallway of this clearly very hastily built prison and nodded their agreement, except one.

"Where's that?" De asked.

"You've never heard of the Underground Kingdom?" Rod gaped at De. He just shook his head.

"Nope. I've only ever lived in Phorbes and now the Great Lands. Not a lot of time for vacations growing up, you know," he said.

It was Mo who decided to explain. "Deep under parts of the Great Lands, the Shadow Lands and Phorbes is a country called the Underground Kingdom. The Kingdom has been ruled by the Rodriguez family for over one hundred years, ever since they and their supporters were exiled from the Golde Continent. Funny thing is, after Golde Continent lost the Global War the Underground Kingdom was all that was left from the old monarchy, so now they're back on top...so to speak."

"Umm...how do they get sunlight? Or water? Or trees?" De questioned.

"We can have a geography lesson later; let's just get out of here!" M interrupted, walking towards the door. The others followed him and they peered outside. They found themselves in a much more complex hallway with doors on either side and around a corner from them.

"Which door?" Mo asked.

"Let's try the stairs instead" M suggested, pointing at the flight of stairs at the end of the hall. The group climbed the stairs and entered the door at the top of them. De stepped in front as they entered the large room with an equally large stained glass window. Around the room were a number of wooden tables and chairs and a serving station; it looked to be a kind of dining facility. A single young man sat at a table near the window, looking out of it instead of at the empty tray in front of him. Even sitting down they could see his dark green, tight fitting t-shirt, similar sized brown pants and a white jacket with a tuft of fur along the hood.

"Who the heck are you?" he looked at the Elementals curiously. His short, curly black hair, light brown skin, and rich accent told the Elementals that he was a native of the Underground Kingdom.

The Elementals tensed themselves for a fight, no doubt sure they could take this single teenager, but Don stepped in front. "We want to join Queen A.G.'s cause. We're here because we want to help."

Everyone looked nervous, but the man in green bought it. "Good! The great A.G. always needs willing aid. I am Del, the overseer of this prison. Come with me, and I'll take you all on a tour of the factory so you will see where you will be stationed." He got up from the table and towards them.

As Del walked towards the door, even Don was surprised at how well his trick was working. They would be led out of the prison by one of A.G.'s henchmen without even lifting a finger. Del passed in between the Elementals and reached for the door, before locking it and turning back to the group.

"How stupid do you think I am?!" he shrieked, looking from person to person. "I remember when you came into the prison, resistance traitors!"

The five of them stepped away from Del and readied themselves for the battle. "It was a good try." Mo told Don, and the latter smiled weakly.

"Now I can personally deliver the Elementals to A.G.! I'll be rewarded like a king!" Del beamed at the thought, speaking so fast that his rolled r's were jumbled with the rest of his speech.

"Good luck taking out all of us, Del! You're outnumbered!" M taunted.

"But how can you beat what you can't catch?" Del smiled maliciously and vanished in a flash of green light.

"Where'd he go?" De searched the room frantically for the villain, who reappeared behind Mo, kicking him hard enough in the side to knock the wind out of him. Before Mo could fight back, Del was gone again.

"He can teleport! We have to make him stay in one place!" Mo cried.

Del reappeared right in De's face. Brandishing a short knife from his jacket pockets, he tried to take a swipe at the Elemental, but De panicked and breathed a burst of fire at Del, causing him to back away from De's flaming mouth. M and Rod rushed forward to continue the attack, but Del disappeared again. Don began searching the room for something to use to help. He found maps and schematics on the nearest table and stuffed them away in his pockets.

"There's got to be some type of weapon here..." he thought aloud, and continued looking.

Del reappeared above M, poised to drop down on the Elemental blade first. Rod saw him and was able to catch the teleporter with a burst of what he believed to be water from behind the serving station. The water pushed Del into a wall, to which Mo followed up by freezing Del in place. He struggled to free himself from the ice and barely dodged the burst M had hurled in his direction. He managed to teleport again at the last second, but reappeared, dazed and confused, in the middle of the floor. Del looked up and threw one of the chairs toward his attackers, barely missing Rod, but catching De. De hit the ground, and Mo flung a few ice shards at Del, which he easily shrugged off. Del gathered himself, ready to teleport again, but was electrocuted and collapsed.

"Good going, M," Rod patted his comrade on the back.

"I'd love to take credit for that, but I didn't do it." M pointed behind Del's crumpled body to Don, hiding behind a table and holding some sort of gun.

"It worked? He's out?" Don called.

"Like a light! Good job!" Mo answered, kicking at Del's collapsed form.

"Yes!" Don yelled, jumping into the air in triumph. "He must have been checking out one of the stun guns I had from the resistance. They're more powerful than I thought," he added, eyeing the contraption in his hands.

"Yes, yes, that's great, but how are we getting out of here?" Rod asked. He stooped down to help De off the ground. The chair hit De hard enough to have him too woozy to move properly.

"Prisoners! Cease all escape attempts and return to your cells!" They turned to hear a group of androids knocking on the locked door. Don looked behind himself at the large window, and back at the Elementals.

"No freaking way," Rod said.

"How far down is it?" M asked.

"Not far!" Mo ran to Don's side and peered out of the window. As the Elementals contemplated their next move, the androids continued yelling and pounding at the door.

"Wha...what's going on?" De asked. His mind was still out of it as well.

"Oh we're just jumping out of a window, let's go guys!" Don motioned towards their escape.

The heavy door finally burst open, but the other Elementals were already racing towards the window. M shot a bolt of electricity at the glass, shattering it.

Rod flung De off of him and out of the window, replaced him with Don, and the five heroes poured out of the window, screaming the entire way out of the prison and down the relatively dirt hill, away from Del's still unconscious body and the still yelling androids.

Rumas Again

The Elementals and Don landed on the ground under the prison with several loud thuds.

"Well, I'm awake now!" De got up from the ground rubbing his backside.

"Thank you, Rod," Don breathed.

"Yeah, just didn't need you breaking your legs or anything," Rod gently let Don down, and as the latter smiled up at his carrier, Mo looked darkly at the both of them.

"HALT ELEMENTAL RESISTANCE!" The heroes looked back up at the window they just jumped out of and saw a small group of androids peering out of it.

"We need to get going before they come after us!" M said in a panic. They ran deeper into the city and turned a few corners to try to lose their metal pursuers. Don and Mo wheezed and coughed from their sprint to shelter, to which Rod only hissed at them to be quiet.

"M, look and see if they're still looking for us," Rod

whispered. M nodded and peeked around the corner of the alleyway.

"ELEMENTAL RESISTANCE! EXPOSE YOURSELF!" One android bellowed as soon as he saw M.

"That answer your question?" M asked. He turned back to the oncoming androids and started firing electricity at them. De moved forward to try to help M hold off their attackers, but Don grabbed his arm.

"Guys! This way!" he said, pointing towards an unmarked door at the end of the alleyway. He stuffed the map in his hand back into his pocket and pointed at the door again. Mo dashed to it and opened it, followed by De and Rod.

"Come on M!" Don called again. M was now fully in the street, blasting at a single android who his electrical powers didn't seem to affect.

"I only got one left! I can take him down!" M answered.

"COME ON!" Don yelled. He went inside the passage he had found, and after a little more complaining, M ran in after him.

"Took you long enough! Come on!" The two ran deeper into the building they had escaped into. They squeezed through a tight hallway and emerged in the remains of a large shop.

"What is this? Where are we, Don?" Mo asked when Don and M emerged from the back of the store.

"Well," Don pulled a map from his pocket. "It *was* the Alcon General Store..."

"What happened to it?" M asked.

The others looked around at the broken shelves, holes in the walls and roof. Nothing intact was on what remained of the shelves. Lights hung broken from the ceiling, torn up aisle markers littered the floor and the checkout lanes had shelves strewn across them. "Looks like it was half-way blown up or something..." Rod said.

"Close. It was ransacked by those metal menaces," a young man emerged from one of the aisles and made the five of them jump. He didn't look to be too much older than they were. "When we didn't give them what they wanted they just started taking it."

"Why are you lurking behind shelves and stuff? You could've given us all a heart attack!" M demanded. The boy ignored him.

"I heard the things outside...are you the Elementals?" he asked.

"Yes, we are. Who are you?" De asked.

"I own what's left of this shop. Well, really my Dad owned it, but now..." he trailed off and looked away from them. The five of them tried their best to avoid each other's eyes; they could all guess how the sudden change in ownership came about.

"If you guys are the Elementals then you guys can fix this. You can make all of this right. That's your job, right? You have to...promise that you will..." the young Alcon boy approached the five of them.

"We...we're gonna do our best," M said, not looking directly at the boy. "But you have to remember, there's only so much we can-"

The shop owner cut M off. There were now real tears behind the strands of his jet black hair as he turned to each of the heroes in turn. "You have to do it. You have to take down A.G. so that we can move on with our lives."

"Yes, I understand that you want justice, but..." M started.

"No...no, *you* don't understand! *You* don't get it! We're all scared to death of that thing...she has those androids killing anybody and everybody...you have to do something!" he wiped his eyes and pointed towards the remains of the front door. "You know what, I think you guys need to leave."

"You have to ignore him, he's young and stupid," Rod started, but the boy kept sniffling and pointing towards the door. The Elementals were obviously no longer welcome in the Alcon General Store. De simply nodded and motioned for the others to walk outside as the owner asked.

"Good job Sparky," Rod said the moment they were outside.

"What did I do?!" M asked.

"That guy probably lost everything, all he probably wanted was a little comfort, something to let him know that his family didn't die in vain," Mo said quietly.

"Hey I was just being realistic! What did you guys want me to do?" M snapped back.

"Lie," Rod and Mo said in unison.

"Sometimes it's good to lie to make people feel better," explained Don. His usually chipper voice was low and serious for once. "People are in pain, their lives are in turmoil. It's you guys' job to fix the people just as much as it's you guys' job to fix the world." De, who remained silent during this exchange, continued to stare into the remains of the general store while M defended himself.

"Well I didn't wanna lie! I mean we might as well be honest with people, and ourselves! We suck; we suck at working together, we barely beat that silver guy, we got beat up and thrown in jail, and the only reason why we got out is because Don had a brain blast. We can't beat A.G. and there is

no need in us acting like we can!" M plopped down on a piece
of debris and looked up at the others. He looked more
frustrated than any of them had ever seen him. "This isn't how
this was supposed to be."

"You guys got me pretending to be a hero in a world
ruled by a crazy robot guard dog; *nothing* is like it's supposed
to be," Rod pointed out.

"Shut up Rod, you know what I mean. We're messing
this thing up way more than we're helping," M responded.

Finally, De turned away from the store and joined the
conversation. "We can't give up," he said simply.

"I love your enthusiasm, I really do, but we really do
suck as heroes," M said.

"Look around you M," De said, gesturing to the
buildings around them, or what was left of them. All around
them were buildings in various stages of destruction: there was
a large fountain with a pair of motionless legs sticking out of it,
a hotel sign with only the "TEL" part remaining, and a headless
statue of what appeared to be the king of the Underground
Kingdom. It looked like they were in the remains of the town's
square. The rest of the group only looked at their surroundings
at the same time M did.

Mo gasped. "Oh wow..." he said from behind his hand.

"They wrecked the place..." M got up from his "seat"
and realized that it was the statue's missing head.

"This could be the whole country if we don't do
something..." De said. "This could be your homes looking just
like this, and your families could end up just like his...or mine,"
he gestured inside to the store owner and then to himself. "I
know what it feels like to have that happen to you, and I don't
want that to happen to anybody else. Even if we mess stuff up,

we can still do a lot of good for people, we just gotta try," De said.

"So what do you suppose we do?" M asked after a moment. The others looked at De as well to hear his answer.

"How should I know, you're the leader, right?" De was challenging M, and he took the bait hook, line, and sinker.

"You're right! If we are to be of any help to the world as Elementals, we need to regroup with the Racksons; they will be able to give us some guidance on how to fix this mess," M started pacing around the square as he spoke.

"Good job," Rod whispered. De grinned quickly so M wouldn't see him.

"Does anyone know how we can get back to Rumas from here?" M asked. He stopped pacing to look at the others.

"Oh! I can help with that!" Don said. He dug back into his pockets and pulled out a map again. "I swiped these from the prison, it should be able to tell us how to get home from here," Excitement was starting to creep back into his voice, an occurrence that De didn't miss.

"So…does this mean we're gonna keep at this?"

"It means we're going home because we have to," M said. He stood on his toes to look at the map with Don. Mo, however, nudged De and nodded his head. De smiled at him.

"Ok, we need to go this way," Don said, pointing to yet another back alley that, according to his map, would lead them to Rumas.

"Here it is!" Don pointed at the top of a hill to the sign marked "To Rumas".

"Finally! I thought we'd never find it," Mo breathed a sigh of relief and began climbing the mound of dirt and rock.

They reached the top and Rod moved the stone door which led to a tunnel.

"It's so dark....oh, thanks De," Don nodded his head at the flame in De's hand lighting their way. At the end of the tunnel Rod moved another stone door, entering into the nighttime environment of southern Rumas. The city was alive with a surprising amount of lights, probably used to make sure any androids patrolling the streets were highly visible.

"What time is it?" M yawned, looking up at the crescent moon in the sky.

"11:42...we'd better turn in for the night, it's been a long day," De suggested. He put out the flame and looked at Mo. "Can we stay at your house tonight?"

"No, you can't," Mo said quickly. Everyone looked at him. "I mean, the house is still bugged probably, the police and androids could be listening to our every move."

"True...what about the Racksons?" M asked.

"They're on the other side of town, it'll be long after midnight before we get-" De was interrupted by Don.

"Hey, you guys can come to my house, its close! It'll be fine; my parents are used to me having people over, Mo stays all the time!" he offered, looking excitedly around at the others.

They all looked at Rod, waiting on him to protest like he did with staying at M's house. Rod looked back at them and smirked.

"At this point I'll sleep at A.G.'s house; I just need sleep."

"Well that settles it, lead the way Don," M nodded.

"Can't sleep?" Don asked. The others had all gone to

bed almost the moment they got to his house, but Don had taken refuge in the kitchen to fix himself a snack after the day he had. He watched Mo creep into the spotless white and black kitchen and sit at the table with him. Don put down his spoonful of ice cream and got up to make Mo some.

"Not too much," Mo said. Don nodded and scooped the dessert into another bowl, slid it to his friend and sat back down.

"So what's up?" He asked.

"Nothing really..."

"Yes there is. You're eating ice cream with me after midnight and not trying to make me put the spoon down; something is wrong," Don pointed out.

"Well you shouldn't be eating this late at night, it won't make you any smaller," Mo said.

Don rubbed his stomach. "It's good so it makes up for it," he got serious again. "But really, what's wrong?"

Mo sighed. "Sometimes I just feel like I don't really fit in with the other guys. I mean, I know we're all Elementals but sometimes it's like I just don't understand them or why they do or say the stuff they do. It's like we're from different planets."

Don scooped out some more ice cream before answering. "Well, aside from the obvious difference-" Don lifted his hand to show his skin. "-you're all different people from very different situations, so of course you're going to be different. But you all have to do what you have to do to beat A.G. Besides, they gave you a nickname. That's a sign you're cool with them,"

"I don't know...I mean yea I guess you're right. I'm still trying to figure out if I like 'Mo' or not but..." Don smiled at Mo, but he didn't return the gesture. Instead he sighed again and continued. "I can deal with everybody else, it's just Rod though; something isn't right with him. He makes me really uncomfortable. Is that wrong?" When Don shook his head Mo continued. "The others are cool, but it's just him. He reminds me so much of those jerks from school," Don nodded and kept eating his ice cream, so Mo ventured even further. "It seems like you guys get along, though..."

Don couldn't stop himself from laughing. He already could tell where Mo was going with his thoughts. "You can't be serious right now." Mo's expression told Don that he was, so Don stopped laughing and continued. "I deal with him, that's it. I mean, have you met him? He's a real...oh hey M!"

Mo turned around and saw the youngest of the group standing in the doorway of the kitchen rubbing his eyes.

"You know you guys should be sleep. We gotta get back to the Racksons tomor-oh ice cream!" M walked a little faster into the kitchen and Don got up to fix him a bowl as well. "Thanks Don, I'll just take a little bit." Don put two scoops in the bowl and slid it to M.

Mo watched him eat the ice cream. "M...when you were studying the history did any of it talk about how older Elementals interacted with each other? Like any word of people fighting or not liking each other?"

M swallowed his mouthful of ice cream as quickly as he could without getting a brain freeze. "Yep. There was a whole chapter in this one memoir book that talked about how much Chabon from the second generation hated their Sync Elemental Mitchell. But they still worked it out and did what they had to do to take down Childress, since Childress had killed Chabon's sister. The duty of an Elemental is to defend the world, no matter what. Sometimes they had to put stuff aside for the greater good," he put down his spoon and raised an eyebrow at Mo. "Why do you ask?"

"No reason. Ok, I'm going to bed now, see you guys in the morning," Mo got up from the table and carried his bowl out of the kitchen.

When Mo was gone M leaned across the kitchen table and spoke to Don. "You might wanna watch him, he may be plotting to get rid of De. Of course, I'd help him, though," M said.

Don laughed. "I'll be sure to keep an eye out for that."

Late the next morning the Elementals awoke to Don's father finishing up a breakfast. They scarfed the meal down the second he finished, and soon Don joined them fitted with the same kind of Skin Armor clothing that he made for the Elementals: a long sleeve orange and white collared shirt and some loose fitting khaki colored pants.

"Hey guys! I hope you got some rest last night, I've been studying this stuff I got from the prison, and it looks pretty major," despite the seeming severity of this news, Don seemed cheerful as usual.

"What is it?" De asked, walking over to peer at the large pieces of paper Don spread out on the table in front of them.

"Well, besides the maps of the whole Underground Kingdom and Rockdale, I also found some schematics for the factory they're building here," Don pointed at the three documents as he explained.

"How does this help?" M asked.

"Well, with these we can figure out how to shut them down! We could go today!" Don explained. The entire room stared at Don for so long that his smile fell. "What?"

"Who told him we were going on a suicide mission?" Rod looked at the others for an answer. Don frowned.

"Don," M started in a pleasant voice. "Are you sure we can handle this? I mean, this is an entire factory we're talking about, with plenty of androids."

"Positive! I mean you guys have been taking out androids left and right and taking the factory down will be fairly simple really; she built the factories just like the haunted toy shop in *The Devil's Toymaker*. I see that movie in my sleep; it'll be a piece of cake taking these places down!"

"We'll take your word for it," Rod said, clearly not having a clue what Don was talking about.

"Well, I think we can do it," De said. "Come on, we saw Rockdale. Do we really wanna take a chance and let that be Rumas or Black City? We gotta try something." When the others all nodded their reluctant agreement De's excitement matched Don's. "Call the Racksons and let's go take Rumas back!" he said. He, Rod, and M headed for the door while Don began stuffing things into a backpack. Don's father spoke before anyone could actually leave.

"Wait," he called.

"What is it Dad?" Don asked.

"If you guys are going to the factory, don't you think your parents should know about it? I'm sure they're worried about you anyway, you should call them." He was speaking directly to M and Rod.

They stopped to contemplate this for a moment. "Can I use your phone?" asked M.

"You wouldn't happen to have another one would you?" Rod asked. Don's father pulled his cell phone from his pocket and handed it to Rod, and the two of them walked with

M to the house phone in the living room. Don left the room and went to find his mother, leaving Mo and De in the kitchen alone.

"I wish I could talk to my Dad," Mo said. "It sucks not having anyone to worry about you."

"Tell me about it," the sound of M trying to explain to his parents that him going to the factory would actually better his future nearly drowned out De's response, but Mo still heard him and felt embarrassed.

"Oh wow, I'm sorry De, I-" Mo looked up at De, who only put up his hand to stop him.

"Jas just put Ma on the phone!" Rod yelled from the living room. De smiled weakly and looked down at Mo.

"Don't worry about it, it is what it is. But look at it this way, at least you know your Dad will be out eventually. At least you have a chance of seeing him again." This really did nothing to help Mo's embarrassment at his words.

"I want to go see my Dad before we go to the factory," he said in almost a whisper.

De nodded. He put his hand on Mo's shoulder but said nothing.

They went through an astounding number of security checkpoints and had to be accompanied by Don's parents and several identity checks to reach Prof. Peters. Rod commented after every one of them that the police were only doing this to give the illusion that they were working. The final checkpoint informed the heroes that only one person was allowed to talk to the prisoner at a time, so they all let Mo go in to talk to his father.

"Morgan...I'm so glad to see you, son," Prof. Peters

looked rather disheveled through the shiny steel bars of his cell. Even if they wanted to break Prof. Peters out there was no way De would've been able to melt these. There were bags under the professor's eyes, he looked as if he hadn't eaten in a little while and the orange and white striped jumpsuit didn't suit him well at all. But in his eyes there was genuine joy at being able to see his son.

"Hi Dad," Mo could see the effect jail was having on his father, and it affected him as well. He stood as close to the bars as he could, and his father did the same. "How...how are you?"

"Oh I'm fine. At the very least this is giving me a chance to catch up on my reading" Prof. Peters smiled sadly, gesturing towards a stack of ragged books in the corner of the cell. None of them looked, at least to Mo, like they would be on his father's reading list.

"That's good, Dad. Hey, at least you'll have some better stories to tell at the dinner table," Mo joked weakly. They both laughed sharply and quickly.

"Son...what's wrong?" he asked gently. Mo chuckled nervously.

"Oh...nothing Dad."

"Morgan what is it?" Prof. Peters asked again, and when his brown eyes met his son's blue ones Mo wanted nothing more than to confess everything to his father. But then he saw the concern in his eyes and folded.

"It's nothing. I'll just be glad when you get out of here. I hope someone can do something about A.G. soon..." Prof. Peters nodded to his son. He reached through the bars to grab his hand but said nothing. Mo smiled weakly and Prof. Peters did the same. He would tell him. Soon.

Prof. Peters' eyes began to shine. "I love you Morgan."

"I love you too, Dad," Mo gave his father's hand a firm squeeze and prepared to leave.

When Mo came back outside from the jail the others all waited for him to speak before addressing him.

"So what's the plan?" he asked.

"Master Rackson and Rose are going to meet us there," M said.

"I've got all the tools I need," Don added, checking his bag.

"I hope you're ready for a big fight," Rod grinned.

"...because we're about to go take out this factory," De finished, looking towards it in the distance.

The Unfinished Factory

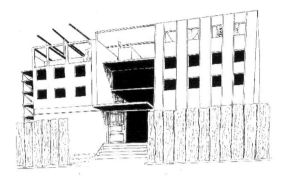

"Kareema Rhama Heximae!" Master Rackson bellowed, utilizing his magical power to blast through two of the androids that were attacking Mo.

"Thanks!" he grinned at his teacher and turned around just in time to dodge an android racing towards him. He looked down at and used the small puddles of water under the android to freeze its fcct to the ground.

"Got another one for you, Rose!" he called over as he ran from the contraption. The Cosmic Elemental ran over and gave it a punch-kick combo powerful enough to break the limbs off its metal form.

Predictably, the unfinished factory was crawling with A.G.'s android servants and more than a few imprisoned humans. As soon as the Elementals approached the outside of the factory they were bombarded by the mechanical menaces, but luckily the Racksons were already there, and once the others arrived they developed a system to take down their enemies.

De was using his new fire breathing ability as if he had had it for years. M and Rod were working together to electrocute and power down the androids. Luckily the Racksons thought to bring a bucket of water, so Rod was able to hit the androids with a burst of water, leaving M to follow up with a quick electric shock; effectively stopping them. Don, who had picked up a reflector shield from the tools he borrowed for the resistance, was making the androids destroy themselves. It seemed as if a new resolve and their imprisonment and escape together had started them on the path to being a real team.

Even Mo was taking out the androids with help from the Racksons. Each time Rod left water on the ground, Mo used it to freeze an android in place; leaving them wide open for either Rose to break with her power infused blows or Master Rackson to use his magical energy to stop. With all of them working together, it didn't take long for the Elementals and Don to clear the outside of the factory.

Master Rackson breathed a sigh of relief and motioned for the others to come closer. "Alright. We have the hard part out of the way, now we can focus on bringing the factory down. Donald, what must we do?"

Everyone turned to Don. "Ok, well thankfully the factory isn't finished yet, so this should be easy. They haven't even started making androids here so all we really have to do is tear the building down,"

"That's it? No crazy plan? I'm disappointed in you Don," M and the others all laughed.

"What about the people inside?" Rose asked.

"Good point, we have to get them out before the place starts coming down," Don agreed. "I'll go."

"I'll come with you," Rose volunteered and the two started walking inside.

"Wait," Master Rackson called. "Rodrik, maybe you should go with them."

"Yeah, I'm sure they could use your help picking a few locks," Mo said.

Rod shrugged. "I'm a little rusty, but it won't take me long to get back in the habit. Besides, you two could use a little more firepower." He picked up his bucket and walked over to join them.

Rose's eyebrows raised "More firepower? What am I then?"

"I just mean-" Rod began.

"Maybe you should stop now," M suggested. Even though Rod listened, it was too late.

"You do realize that I'm just as capable as any of you? That I've done this before, right? I see I'm going to have to show you something..." Rose snapped, walking away from the others and into the factory. "I'll see you when everyone is freed," she yelled over her shoulder. Don and Rod exchanged a look and ran after her.

"Try to be careful," Master Rackson called to them.

"So...what do *we* do?" M asked.

"We should give them a little head start. We have to make sure the prisoners are out of harm's way before the place starts crumbling," Mo answered. He reached into his pocket and removed one of the handheld weapons his father had created.

Everyone nodded their agreement. "Let's take the city back," Master Rackson said, and he led his students inside the factory.

The factory was huge on the inside. Just as the plans Don stole had indicated; the factory was three stories tall, metallic on the outside and cold and dark looking on the inside.

The first floor consisted of a huge assembly line and conveyer belt in which the androids were put together. Since this factory wasn't yet completed, the assembly line was obviously missing parts, but all of them could see just how huge it would be. Rooms to the sides were where the various parts were designed and held before being brought to the center assembly room. The stairs in the middle of the floor led upstairs to the training and programming area on the second floor.

Don's stolen blueprints told them that the second floor was built with enough space for androids to be programmed to serve A.G., and by extension the Pru Empire, and for them to gain the battle prowess needed to do it by force. The third floor was living quarters for the humans who ran the factory; too far from the ground for them to safely jump out of the small windows. Signs that Rose, Don and Rod were already fighting their way to the third floor were evident. There were a few dismantled androids spread across the first floor, and loud clatter came from above them. Moments later a large group of people raced down the stairs and out of the building. None of them paid any attention to the Elementals on the first floor; they were focused only on their new freedom.

"Well, let's get started!" De giddily started a blaze at the large assembly line of the first floor. M countered by finding the power source and short circuiting it. Mo, however, left his comrades and ran towards the rooms along the side of the first floor. He kicked one of the doors, and it flung open to reveal a room full of android parts.

He picked up one of the android's laser hands from the floor and smiled. "I'm going to destroy the parts so they can't make any more androids!" He announced, and practically skipped off into the room.

Master Rackson focused his attack on the outer walls of the building. Summoning concentrated blasts of magical energy from his fingertips, the old master sent blasts exploding into each wall they hit. After successfully disrupting all electrical capabilities on the first floor, M ran up to the second floor where the android programming software was. The three downstairs heard several large "Kabooms" signifying that M was successful in overloading the androids' computer "brains."

After about fifteen more minutes of this destruction, Mo ran back out of the rooms and rejoined De and their teacher. "This is pretty fun, huh?"

"No...this is wrong..." Master Rackson stopped his attack and signaled for De to do the same.

"What do you mean? I mean, this is like payback for everything they've put us through," De said.

"No...it's too quiet. I don't hear Rose or any of the others anymore," Master Rackson pointed out.

"Oh crap...ok let's go see what's happening," De agreed. The three started walking towards the stairs just as Del and the Silver Man appeared at their peak.

"What are you doing here?" De demanded.

"Our jobs, hothead. Did you really think Queen A.G. would leave one of her factories undefended?" Del asked "We're the defenders."

"You two know each other?!" Mo stammered.

The Silver Man just rolled his eyes and shook his head just enough for him to notice Master Rackson. "You..." he said. His eyes burned with a pure hatred, but Master Rackson said nothing to him.

"So, will you three come quietly for Queen A.G.'s judgment, or will we have to beat you like we did your friends?" Del threatened. De shot a flame that only barely missed his head as an answer. "Have it your way then."

Del teleported directly in front of Master Rackson and engaged the elder in hand to hand combat. Luckily, he was able to stop Del with a swift and strong blast of magical energy. Del flew backwards into a wall and teleported away before Master Rackson could commence the beat down.

The Silver Man leapt from the balcony and turned his hands into large swords, chasing Mo down with them. Mo stopped firing his laser hand and ran backwards away from the dual wielding shape shifter...directly into a corner. De ran upstairs to try to find the others but was quickly stopped by Del teleporting in front of him. This, however, freed up Master Rackson to save Mo from being impaled. He used his power to move a piece of the destroyed wall in between the two combatants, and the Silver Man got his blades stuck in it.

"Thanks again!" Mo called, and ran to the top of the stairs to help De fight off Del. Master Rackson took one last look at the Silver Man struggling to remove his (now hands) from the wall and headed for the battle on the second floor. He had almost reached the stairs when he felt a hand tighten around his waist; the Silver Man was free and had extended his arms to constrict Master Rackson.

"We're not done," the Silver Man spat, snatching Master Rackson back towards him.

Atop the stairs, Del was teleporting at top speed, attempting to dodge both De and Mo's various attacks and stab at them with his daggers. He slipped up and appeared in front of De just as he was trying out his fire breathing ability once again.

"Ah!" Del yelled, frantically trying to put out his flaming

white jacket.

"What's-a matter, Del? Too hot? Let me cool you down!" Mo taunted him. Del teleported again, but didn't immediately reappear.

"Where'd he go?" De wondered.

The Silver Man and Master Rackson were in a dead heat battle on the first floor. The Silver Man was busy trying to smash Master Rackson with one of his hands currently shaped like a mallet, but the surprisingly nimble spell caster dodged every swing. As Master Rackson tried to hit the Silver Man with magical energy, he deflected each blast with his other, shield shaped hand. De and Mo ran downstairs to try to turn the tide of the battle, with De throwing fire as he ran. This forced the Silver Man to turn his attention and his shield towards the two of them and block the attacks, but also left him open to Master Rackson.

"Kareema Rhama Heximae!" Master Rackson bellowed, unleashing a blast powerful enough to send the Silver Man flying into the open door of one of the parts rooms when it connected. De and Mo cheered, but Master Rackson just shook his head. "I appreciate that, but go find the others. We have to get out of here, quickly."

The two nodded and headed back up the stairs. They were stopped once again by a reappearing Del, wearing a new brown jacket and an angry expression.

"I'm done playing with you people! Time for my good trick..." Del snarled. He lifted up his left hand as if to say stop, but nothing happened. De and Mo laughed.

"Am I supposed to be scared because you said 'stop'?" Mo asked. He started to run past Del, but he smirked and fired a remarkably strong blast of ki energy. It seemed that in addition to his teleportation power, Del had also mastered the very Elemental-like ability to turn his body's kinetic energy into a powerful blast.

The green burst of power traveled through the air much like the android's laser blasts, and the intensity of the attack sent Mo rolling back down to the first floor. He landed on his back; clearly unconscious from both the close range attack and his tumble down the stairs.

"No, no!" De yelled, running down after Mo's body. Master Rackson also ran to Mo's side, but was distracted by the Silver Man's mallet arm launching out of the parts room at him. He dodged the strike and watched the Silver Man emerge from the room. He backed into De trying to revive Mo and whispered to him as he kept his eyes on the two villains closing in on them.

"Derren, listen to me, I have a pla...Derren?" Master Rackson looked up to see De shooting flame after flame at Del, who only laughed and teleported in and out of the way. Master Rackson tried to stop the remaining Elemental, but the Silver Man once again sent his extending arms after him, this time constricting Master Rackson completely with it, leaving him helpless to stop Del from teleporting behind De and hitting him with a ki blast that sent him to meet Mo on the floor.

The Silver Man slung Master Rackson across the room and he and Del approached the old master as he got to his knees, watching the two walk towards him.

"Are you ready to join the others Elemental? You prepared to see the end come for your little resistance? Do you know that Queen A.G. has now won?" The Silver Man let Del overtake him, hanging back and letting him keep talking.

"Maybe your death will be quick, but hopefully she'll make you suffer," Del continued. The Silver Man stretched out one of his hands to the point where it was large and flat enough to resemble a giant spatula.

"Who knows? Maybe Queen A.G. will turn you over to the two of us. We'll be her new favorites once we bring all of you in. I can think of a few things I would do to you people. Like maybe..."

But what exactly Del would do to the captured Elementals Master Rackson never found out, for at that moment the Silver Man swung his flattened hand directly at Del, striking him across the head and knocking him unconscious instantly.

Master Rackson watched this clear betrayal with mild amusement. He got to his feet and dusted himself off before addressing the Silver Man. "He is certainly irritating. What will you tell him when he awakens?"

The Silver Man shrugged. "You have vast magical powers, we all know that. I'll just say you must have done something magical."

"Fair enough," Master Rackson replied. He stepped over Del to get closer to the Silver Man. "Would it do any good to attempt to change your mind?"

The Silver Man shook his head. "I'm too far gone now."

"I understand."

"You know what I have to do now, right?" The Silver Man asked

"Take me. Leave them" Master Rackson said simply.

"I'll need more than just you to make it believable," the Silver Man pointed out, tossing his locs to one side.

"Take Rose as well; She'll understand when she wakes

up. Which reminds me, how could you-" Master Rackson began.

"I didn't do it, he did," the Silver Man gestured towards Del's body. "You guys were doing a number on this place. One of those androids sent a distress signal out, and A.G. got word of it. She was upset so he got nervous and just went around blasting people before I could calm him down."

"Understandable, but all the more reason why you should take us and leave the children."

The Silver Man laughed. "Taking you two away from them would be just as good as taking them to A.G. myself. They won't survive without you two."

Master Rackson looked over the Silver Man's shoulder at De and Mo. "They will. I have faith in them," he looked back at the Silver Man and grinned. "Besides, they beat you once and were going to beat you again, so they will be fine."

"You and I both know full well I was holding back. In a real fight, I would've killed them."

"Yes, yes, that's what all the 'bad guys' say. Either way, my answer remains the same: Take Rose and me and leave the children. Oh, but get them out of here please, the reinforcements should be here at any moment," he noticed the Silver Man's expression at this request and continued. "Unless of course, you would like me not to go quietly, and I'm sure you and I both know full well how that would turn out."

The Silver Man sneered. "I'm not like I was back then. But fine, I hope you know what you're doing."

"I do," Master Rackson's tone oozed the confidence he had placed in his students. "Well, get on with it then."

Master Rackson lifted his head and stuck out his chest, ready for the blow. The Silver Man readied his hand again. "I'm not sorry, you know," he said.

"I know."

The Silver Man whacked Master Rackson's face full force and he too, fell in a heap on the floor. Right before he lost consciousness, he managed to see the Silver Man stoop down to heave Mo on his shoulders.

New Leadership

"Man my head hurts," De got up from the ground and looked around. He was surprised to be surrounded not by a wrecked building, but trees. "Wait, where am I?"

"Good question," Rod agreed. He too had regained consciousness in this strange clearing. "Did we get got again?"

The others started to awake as well, but it was Don who finally figured out the mystery. "I recognize this place; we're in those woods outside Cirix, close to Rivera. That factory is right around the corner; somebody must've brought us here!"

"But who?" De questioned, as Don moved to help Mo get up.

"Who knows, who cares, as long as we're all here," M said.

"But we're not...where are the Racksons?" Mo asked.

M leapt to his feet. "We have to go get them, they may still be inside! Or worse!"

The others agreed and ran back to what was left of the factory. The top floors seemed to have collapsed upon each other, and the rubble was littered with small electrical flames. Silently, all five of them hoped that the Racksons had not been inside.

"Call them," De suggested.

M nodded and Don handed him his cellphone (he was the only one of them with one). M dialed the number for Rackson Manor and let the phone ring. No answer.

"Don't suppose there's any way they're like at the store or something is there?" Don tried to keep the mood light. It didn't work.

"So what now?" Mo asked after a moment.

"We should finish the plan, that way we can beat A.G. and then-" Don began.

"Nonsense. We have to save the Racksons, who knows what A.G. is putting them through. We will go find A.G. and bring them back!" M interjected.

"But...we can't possibly beat A.G. right now, and even if we did, we would still need to get rid of the fac-" Don continued, but M cut him off again.

"Who is this we? Look Don, I understand that you want to help, but this is not your concern-"

"Don't do it," Rod warned M.

"-this is a job for Elementals. Things have gotten serious and seeing as how you aren't an Elemental-" he continued.

"Stop dude," De pleaded. He could see Don and Mo getting angry.

"-you should just leave this to the real heroes," M finished anyway. He turned to the other three to address them. "Now, team..."

Don was apparently too upset to formulate a good response, and only walked away from the group to another part of the clearing. Mo, however, had something to say on his behalf.

"If you send Don home, I'm going too." There was none of the usual softness in his voice.

"Don't be ridiculous Mo, *you* are an Elemental," M said, barely looking at him.

"So? Elemental or not, Don's been a hell of a lot of help to us! He beat Del, told De how to free us from jail, and told us how to take down the factory! We need him, and I'm not gonna be around if we don't have him because who knows what'll happen!"

None of them had ever heard Mo curse before, so even something as mild as that was enough of a shock to silence everyone. Mo had started walking to Don's side when M grabbed his arm.

"Look Mo, I understand that you're loyal to him, but at this point we can't afford to take any more chances. You guys need to trust the judgment of your leader-"

"Man, get it through your hard head, YOU AIN'T A LEADER! Everything you've tried to get us to do SUCKED. So shut up, sit down, and listen to us before you get us all killed!" Rod's outburst was nowhere near as shocking as Mo's but just as effective. When M rounded on him, Mo snatched out of his grip and stood beside Don, away from their "leader."

"And I guess I'm supposed to listen to you, Rod? The thug?"

"At least I'd keep us from getting killed!"

"Yeah, right before you do it yourself for a profit!" Rod's eyes bulged at the idea, but he refused to stop arguing.

"Dude you need to get over yourself! Just because you knew the Racksons first doesn't mean jack. You were ready to give it all up back in Rockdale, and now all of a sudden you wanna try to be in charge again? Naw. Face it dude, you ain't got a clue how it works in the real world!"

"I don't know the real world? I know plenty!" M argued back.

"Yeah right! You wouldn't last a second on your own without people like me around, you uppity lil-"

"What? WHAT?" M, though he was much shorter than Rod, ran up to him, fully ready to fight him. When De jumped between the two their fighting only got worse.

"Come on guys! This is not the time to be fighting!" Mo yelled over M and Rod's continued argument and De's struggle to keep them separated. Don looked on with mild interest but said nothing to stop or encourage the fight.

"You shut up too! You ain't much better than him!" Rod snapped. He freed himself from De's grip and waited for Mo's response but nothing was said. Mo just glared at him.

"Look, if me being around is gonna cause all this drama I'll just leave!" Don said. He had already started backing away from the other four when Mo grabbed him.

"And if he goes, I go!" Mo said. This time M agreed with Rod and both gave a loud "So?"

"Okay whoa whoa hold up! We're taking this way too far!" De said. "We can't split up like this, we still gotta-"

"Will you stop trying to take my job!" M yelled.

"He's doing a better job at it than you are, he probably should have it!" Mo snapped back. "We all think he should anyway!"

At Mo's words a silence fell upon the five boys. Mo, Don, and Rod all looked towards De, all thinking the same thing. M stared at him too, but his face was filled with nothing but disapproval. At the center of all this, De could do nothing but mouth one word: "What."

"Him? What is he gonna do? He barely even understands what it means to be an Elemental. He's only been around a few weeks!" M argued.

"He knows more about how to survive from those few weeks than you learned in a year, so who cares?" Rod looked directly at M; daring him to argue more.

"Well, since I'm not an Elemental I don't know how much my vote counts, but I vote De too!" Don also looked at M as he spoke, but M didn't meet his gaze and instead kept looking to Rod.

"You still didn't say what he could do. I know all there is to know about our history as Elementals, I know the Racksons the best, I-"

Rod cut him off. "-almost got us killed on that mountain, always bring up stuff to make us fight, and are an overall ass."

M looked to each of the others for some type of reassurance or someone to disagree with what Rod was saying, but when he found none he went to a patch of grass and sat down away from everyone else.

"Umm...ok, while this is all nice and stuff, how about asking the guy who this conversation is about?" De finally spoke up.

Don smiled. "You had to have known this was coming. You always have the best advice for us, and what you tell us to do almost always works out."

"But-"

"I know I'd feel a lot better if *you* were calling the shots," Mo agreed.

"Guys, I don't know..."

"You can't be any worse than that," Rod assured him, gesturing towards M pouting in the grass. "So what do you say?"

De took a second to think about it. Yes he had done pretty well at keeping up with the other guys, but being in charge? Of the last hope of their country? It seemed like way too much for him...

"I'm not really the 'leader' type..." Even as he began the sentence he could see M get excited. If he didn't accept the position now who knew where they would end up. "But-" he took a deep breath. "I'll do what I can. At least until we save the Racksons," as soon as De said the words M put his head in his hands. At the very least, he had shut him up. The other three looked to De to see what their next move would be.

"What?" he asked.

"Where are we going? Are we going to go save the Racksons, or are we going to stick to the first plan?" Mo asked.

"Oh...um, well, Don was right, we can't fight A.G. now. We have to cut off her factories and stuff," De felt like he already wasn't doing a good job as leader, but Mo beamed at him.

"Good call. We might can handle the big boss lady if we take out her factories. But are we really gonna be able to handle this without the Racksons? Just being honest," Rod asked.

De's natural confidence was shining through now. "Of course we can. We just have to work together more, and better. Besides, we already took out one,"

Rod raised his eyebrows. "But that factory wasn't even finished and we still kinda got got. What're we gonna do against a full one?"

"That's where I come in," Don said, patting his backpack. "I snatched floor plans for the other factories when we were in the unfinished one. They were probably using them to make sure that all the factories were equal. Anyway, I can find a way for us to shut the others down with these," Mo and Rod both looked satisfied.

M raised his head to add his own complaints. "Do your plans have a location for these other factories? Or a way to beat Del and that silver guy? Or A.G. for that matter? I'm still seeing a lot of issues."

"Well, most people are still hiding out here, so there's really no one to ask..." De started, and M smirked. "If I remember right though, Rivera is like twenty miles that way, so we might as well go and ask around there. And for that other stuff, we just gotta go for it. You know, have faith and stuff." De answered. It was a mark of how determined the others were to agree with De that no one complained about the walk this time.

"Yeah, when we get to Rivera I can try and see if we can figure out where the other factories are," Rod added.

"Don and I can start figuring out how we'll beat those guys too. With both of our minds working they won't stand a chance!" Mo piped in.

M muttered something along the lines of "reckless" and "improper planning" but raised no more questions. Confident that the others would work with him much more than they worked with M, De seemed pretty pleased with himself. "Ok, sound good everyone?"

"Yep!" They answered.

"Well, it's getting kinda late. Don can we crash at your house again and head to Rivera in the morning?" De asked.

"Sure! My parents will love that!" Don beamed.

"Welp, looks like we have a plan! Let's get this started

everyone!" De ran ahead of them, towards their next destination, with Rod, Mo and Don right behind their new leader and M sulking after them.

Water and Ice

"I'm telling you, I don't know anything!" Rod gave his "informant" a hearty shove against the wall to get out more of the truth out of him.

"Wrong again buddy. I think you do know more. Tell me where the factories are!" Rod looked a bucket of water he "borrowed" from the river and doused his informant with it. However, instead of sputtering and confessing like Rod expected, he started to spark under the waves.

"Whoa! You're an android?!" He jumped back and the android hit the ground. Rod looked at this android he had been threatening strangely. It had a skin tone similar in shade to his own instead of the metallic color of the androids. This android wore clothes that Rod had seen on shelves back home and even had what looked like black hair visible from under the hat on its head.

"Elemental, you will pay for your rebellion against Queen A.G.!" The android threatened, but it seemed like Rod's dousing was affecting its motor skills. It launched insults at Rod, but didn't get up from the ground.

"No way dude, this just got a lot better," Rod laughed. He grabbed the android by the collar and started dragging it back to the abandoned apartment where the others were waiting for him.

The entire town of Rivera was built on a portion of the giant river that ran through much of the Great Lands. Buildings were scrunched together on manmade islands in this section of the river, and to keep up with the aquatic feel of the town the only ways to get from one island to the other was by the constantly running boat system or to use the underwater tunnels that connected some of the islands. The town took in hosts of tourists thanks to its location and attractions, and the money in the town was reflected in the expensive architecture. Compared to the more urban locales like Rumas where skyscrapers were on nearly every corner and the farming community of Center City, Rivera looked like something out of a dream; a quaint little town built over a body of water. Of course, the beauty of the town was tainted by the presence of A.G.'s soldiers stomping around the islands, and though one could fairly easily look through any of the islands the Elementals had still been unable to find any new information.

They had spent the last three days trying to find out where the next factory was, interrogating everyone they thought might know something. Since intimidation was Rod's strong suit, they had allowed him to do most of that. The five had been working out of an abandoned apartment that Don found, but even with Rod harassing everyone they met, the group hadn't had any real success until this very moment. It was a fact that Rod's android informant made sure to remind him of.

"Foolish Elemental! I bet your kind can't even find the

factories you want to know so much about! You'll never be able to defeat Queen A.G.!" As Rod dragged the android through the streets on the main island of the city, he began to regret his decision to leave it functioning.

"Shut up you can opener. Or better yet keep talking. I'm gonna see if Don can make you say something useful," Rod finally arrived at the door of their temporary hideout and kicked it open. "Honeys, I'm home! And I brought a friend!" He announced.

M jumped up from the dining room table, but he saw Rod dragging the android and stopped. "Who did you-what are you doing?!"

"Getting info," Rod told him. He mustered the rest of his strength and slung the android into the middle of the room.

"Rod!" De yelled. Once the android hit the ground with hollow clang instead of a more human-like thud, he looked relieved, then confused. "This is an android?!"

Rod nodded. "Don, this guy knows stuff, but he won't spill. Can't you open him up and make him?" Rod jumped over the back of the couch and landed with a soft plop on the cushions.

Mo walked around the still motionless but very talkative android and confronted the Water Elemental. "Rod...do you know how dangerous it is to bring an android here? What if it attacks? Or calls in reinforcements?" Mo's voice was dripping with disapproval at Rod's actions.

"We all agreed we were going to let Rod take the lead on this one," De reminded him. He had stooped down to look at the android with Don. "We are literally in his element," he gestured out of the window, from which they could see the river.

Don had busied himself down at the android's side. He moved the android's face and felt its chest before he opened the cavity to reveal a number of wires and circuitry. De backed away at this point; the sight of this very human looking creation with an open chest was a little too much for him. M, however, was intrigued and took De's spot beside Don checking the android's wiring. Predictably, the android didn't like that. "Get away from me, resistance scum!"

"Mouthy, isn't he?" De yelled over the android's continued protests to Don's inspection.

"Nearly talked me to death on the way over here. Took everything I had not to just destroy it right there," Rod admitted.

"What do you think Don?" Mo asked after a moment.

Don put a finger up but said nothing. He left the room and came back with his backpack and pulled out a few tools. When they had gone back to his home for the night he filled his backpack with as many of his engineering tools as he could so that he would be prepared for any situation he could think of. "Don't touch me!" The android screamed. "Queen A.G. will have your heads for this! She will not take kindly to her loyal servants being attacked!"

"Shut up, dude. The good guys have you now," M kicked the android in agitation. "So why does he look...real?" He added to the others.

Don finally spoke. "He was made differently from the others, it seems like whoever A.G. has working in the factories now must be pretty smart to doctor up Prof. Peters' original design. This one is made more like Lauryn: to blend in. I would guess that this guy here was like a spy." Don pulled a small touch screen device from his pocket and inserted it into the android's chest, effectively (and finally) shutting the complaining machine up. He then began pushing and swiping the screen of his device.

"My dad's design was fine as it was..." Mo muttered.

"Too good, if you ask me," Rod added. Mo rolled his eyes.

"Ok! That should do it. Ask him a question, anyone," Don said after a minute.

"What's your name?" M blurted.

"I am Android 5621-X. The covert name I use is Larry," the android replied in a monotone.

"So you basically gave him a truth serum?" Mo asked

"Basically. It was pretty simple actually; you remember when Dr. Exot had to do the same thing in *Ever Stars*?"

"Oh yea! It took him forever," Mo said.

"Right!" I'm actually shocked it was this easy for me-"

De cleared his throat. "Oh, right. Ask him anything else, you guys," Don leaned back on the floor and encouraged the others to ask questions.

"How many of you androids are there?"

"Where are the Racksons?"

"How much do you hate your job?"

"You got an android girlfriend?"

"There are over 2000 currently functioning androids serving under Queen A.G., but the resistance continues to lessen that number. I do not know who these Racksons of which you speak are, but most prisoners are taken directly to Queen A.G. I was created only to serve Queen A.G., if that is to be called my job. I do not have what you refer to as a 'girlfriend', but I do share a special bond with Android 3217,"

Larry the android replied to Mo, M, De, and Rod's questions in turn.

"I never thought an android would know what a girlfriend was...you really ain't like the others, are you?" Rod asked.

"No. I was made for reconnaissance; to make it easier to spread Queen A.G.'s regimen. Queen A.G. must know how to infiltrate the rest of the world stealthily," Larry replied. Silently Don patted himself on the back.

"Makes sense. The rest of the world will be prepping for an A.G. invasion, so she has these guys casing the other continents to take them over from the inside," Rod figured.

"Where are the other factories?" M asked.

"One is here, in Rivera. One is in Grandia, and one in Rockdale," Larry replied.

"Well we did right in coming here," M nodded. De grinned at him, and he realized he had inadvertently given De a compliment. "I would have suggested the same."

Mo was the next to ask a question. "Where is the factory here?"

Larry's eyes (one of the few things it could still move) looked right at Mo. "It is under the river; near Eris Island."

De, M, Rod, and Mo all exchanged shocked looks. Don, however, nodded and started rummaging through his bag. He emerged, snatched his handheld device out of Larry, and returned to his bag.

"How are we supposed to get underwater? I can't even swim! Who would build a factory...what are you looking for?" De interrupted himself when Don's searching got louder.

"My navigation tool," Don said from inside his bag. "It, combined with the map of the factory I have should tell us where under the river-HERE!" he said, and emerged with the circular object.

"Even if we know where under the river the factory is, how do you propose we get there to destroy it?" M questioned.

"We could get a submarine," De suggested. When the others looked at him, he clarified. "I mean, the people and androids have to have a way to get there without drowning, so we just find what they have and use it to get there."

"Sounds good to me," Rod agreed.

De nudged him. "You realize that *you* will probably have to steal the sub, right?"

"I figured. Are you sure you tryna make me a good guy?"

"What about Larry?" Mo interrupted, pointing at the now deactivated android. "Should we bring him with us, you know, for extra firepower?"

"He's an android designed for reconnaissance Mo, he doesn't have firepower. Plus, it would be more trouble than its worth for me to try to fix him. I think we could just leave him here, turned off," Don explained.

"That's fine with me, lets head to the river already. I'm ready to get out of this rat trap," M shot a small bolt of electricity at a small rodent in the corner, sending it scurrying back into its home.

"You heard the kid, let's go to the river," De said, and led the way out of the house.

Eris Island was the southernmost island in the group of them that made up Rivera. It was also one of the most popular because of the water park and huge aquarium on it, as well as the beachfront that was at its tip. Ever since A.G.'s androids took over, tourism became almost non-existent in Rivera, so a visit to the waterfront wasn't romantic or relaxing anymore since androids were crawling around the place. The restaurants around the beach were long since abandoned, and the once bustling area was a ghost town; except for A.G.'s henchmen boarding a submarine to the factory.

"Stop them!" De yelled.

The androids heard him, and moved much quicker to avoid battle. De started shooting flames at the submarine's exterior as the machine dove under the water. De turned to his comrades; Don, of course, could do nothing but stare back, and M and Rod did the same knowing that their powers wouldn't be able to affect such a large object or body of water. Mo tried to freeze the water around the sub, but only ended up solidifying the top part of the river. De sighed and sat down on the man-made beach.

"Now what do we do, O Great Leader?" M asked. De ignored his sarcasm and answered seriously, at least at first.

"Somebody's gotta go after it and bring the sub back so the rest of us can ride it down. Unless you've got one tucked away in your 'fro."

Rod nodded and stepped forward. "You could've just asked, you know."

"I wanted to leave it up to your brilliant mind to figure out," De answered, grinning at Rod.

"Why does he get to go?" Mo asked.

"Because he's the only one of us that won't drown. He controls water in case you forgot," M explained.

"Well, I could go with him," Mo offered.

Rod raised an eyebrow. "And what's gonna keep you

from drowning? You may be alright with ice and all, but when it comes to the wet stuff that's my territory."

Mo however, looked determined. "I can freeze a helmet of the water around my head. I'd probably have to keep freezing it on the way down, but it should work long enough for me to follow you."

"Well if that's the case, you could do that for everybody," Rod pointed out.

Mo shook his head. "I...I don't think I could constantly keep up four of them. I know I could do one."

Rod looked around at the others. De and Don nodded their approval and M just shrugged. "Fine," Rod relented. "But you had better not get in my way," he walked towards the edge of the water with Mo right behind him.

"Be careful down there, you two. If the two of you get overwhelmed send us some type of signal," De advised. M muttered "And what would we do?" behind him, but was ignored.

"This is so awesome!" Don said. "This is just like the episode of *Sea Kid* when he and his sidekick had to swim to the Ocean Oasis..."

"Yeah, I'm gone!" Rod shouted. He dove into the river, and after freezing some water on his head, so did Mo.

The two swam for nearly fifteen minutes before they caught up to the submarine. Mo stopped and pointed happily at it, leading Rod to smack him in the back. They swam closer and eventually found an emergency exit hatch on the submarine's outside. Rod opened it and they went inside.

"Why'd you hit me?" Mo said as soon as his ice helmet was off.

"Shut up or I'll do it again. We have to get control of this place," Rod used his powers to suck the water off of their clothes and motioned for Mo to be quiet and follow him.

The interior of the submarine was fairly straightforward: a long gray hallway that led the boys directly from the emergency exit, past the machinery and to a heavy metal door that no doubt lead to the deck. Rod peeked in the glass window on it.

"Ok, there's six androids inside; one driving the submarine, so he'll have to be last. Are you ready to stay out of my way so I can do this?"

Mo frowned at him. "I can help, you know."

"You never helped with the androids before, but whatever," Rod spun the wheel shaped latch on the door and flung it open. "So this is my ship now," he informed the androids that turned to face him. The android piloting the submarine barely turned away from the controls as he sent the other five to fight Rod and Mo. Immediately, they started firing laser blasts at him and Mo, but the two managed to duck behind some of the control panels on the deck to avoid them. One of the blasts went wayward and hit the hull of the sub, allowing some water to flow in before the commander sent an android to the hole to plug it with his hand.

"Stop! You'll sink the submarine and we shall all be destroyed!" he ordered.

"Smart move," Rod smirked. "Too bad I can still use my powers," he flung the water on the deck at the android nearest to him, pushing him backwards. The others rushed forward, ready to engage Rod when Mo emerged from behind him, freezing the water under the androids. The frozen floor made the androids slip and fall, but also cracked the bottom of the sub. The commanding android looked over his shoulder in a panic.

"Stop, stop! You'll doom us all! What do you want Elementals?" he slammed the ship to a halt and turned to face them.

Rod smiled. "I told you, I want the sub. I'm gonna take it back to the surface, and you guys are gonna get out of it and never come back."

"Never! We will never abandon our posts!" the android argued.

"And if I don't get this ship, you won't have to ever leave your post, isn't that right Mo?" Mo looked at Rod, clearly confused. Rod nudged him and pointed at the water still on the floor.

"Oh!" Mo finally understood and froze more of the ship's floor, creating even more cracks in the frame.

"You seem like one of the smart androids like our buddy Larry. You can see that it's either my way or you all die, right?" Rod threatened as Mo continued to crack the floor of the sub. A few drops of water started to seep inside below them as he spoke.

The other androids looked to their leader. He seemed to indeed be a "smart" android, as he took a moment to contemplate the situation. "Take the ship! It is yours!" he said finally.

"Kinda sucks to have human intelligence now, doesn't it? Self-perseverance is a pain," Rod laughed, motioning for the androids to line up against the wall.

"They've been gone a while..." Don mentioned.

"We just have to trust that they're alright," De assured him. M muttered something under his breath. "What did you say?" De rounded on him.

"I said that if you were a real leader you would've found a way to go with them, so you wouldn't have to 'trust that they're alright'," he looked right back at De.

"Well if you feel so strongly about it, why didn't you try to go with them?"

"I'm not leader anymore, am I?"

De sighed heavily. "Look M, I know that being in charge was your thing, but the other guys..." he looked at Don for support, who nodded. "...had to do what they thought was best for all of us. I didn't ask for this, you know? So why don't you stop blaming me for it? We're not gonna get anywhere if we're always at each other's throats. The rest of us have been doing good at working together, you gotta do the same."

M stared at him for a while. "For the sake of the team, I'll do what needs to be done, nothing more and nothing less." He got up from their spot at the edge of the water and walked to another part of the beach.

De and Don looked at each other, the latter just shrugged. "It's a start, I guess," De looked back the water, wondering if the other two were faring any better.

"Whoa, whoa, what're you doing?" Rod snatched the wheel from Mo. The androids had been frozen to the wall and were forced to watch the two Elementals fight over who would drive the ship.

"I'm going to drive the sub," Mo said simply. "You're doing fine intimidating them, but this is where *I* come in!" he snatched the wheel away from Rod with some effort.

"No way am I letting you drive this thing!" Rod said.

"Do you think I can't do it or something?" Mo said, his

voice rising.

"You probably do know *how* to drive it, I just don't trust you doing it," Rod clarified.

"Really? The criminal doesn't trust me...that's funny."

Rod's eyes narrowed. "You can't even hold your own in the easiest fight; I can't trust you to have my back on dry land, how can I put my life in your hands underwater? Just like I said back in Rumas, you ain't no better than Sparky. Neither one of you are cut out for this life; you probably even worse than him. You'd of been better off on land with the others, or better yet, back at home." He snatched the wheel and pushed Mo out of his way.

Mo was absolutely livid by this point; his voice rose as he stared at Rod's back. "You know what? You're just like those kids at school. You think you know everything and can do everything just because what, you have girls? Because people know your name? You can't be trusted to make good decisions, you can't make good decisions about your life, look at it! You barely got out of jail with just you and one other person, how can I believe you'll keep all five of us out of danger?" Mo stood in front of the wheel and in front of Rod, forcing him to look at the Ice Elemental.

Rod stared at him for a second and his hand left the wheel of the sub. For a second Mo thought that he had won the argument, and then Rod's fist came flying at him. Mo's hands went up, but did little to stop Rod from connecting with his face. Mo stumbled backwards from the blow, and against all good judgment charged at Rod. Rod easily shoved him off of him, but Mo didn't try to fight him anymore. Rod stepped directly into Mo's face. The two met eyes before Rod started talking.

"I never liked you. You have your entire life handed to you and the second things start to go wrong you crumble. You can't even stand up and tell your old man about the best thing about you. You're weak and I hate weak dudes. So get out of my way punk, and let me do this."

"I don't like you either," Mo said through gritted teeth. "You're just a bully, like everyone else. Just treating me like crap because you think you're better than me or something. You don't understand anything about what I deal with! Just because you think you're cool, and people like you..."

It was obvious that neither would be backing down anytime soon. Rod opened his mouth to continue arguing, leaving the androids still frozen to the wall behind them to watch the spectacle in front of them.

"Look! I see something coming out of the water!" Don yelled, pointing at the water's surface. Sure enough, after nearly an hour underwater the submarine was rising to the top again. The hatch opened and out toppled the captured androids, their hands bound with several layers of ice. They spat several curses at the heroes, but with their hands frozen together they were unable to do much else, especially considering one of them seemed to be missing an entire arm.

"Wow, looks like Rod and Mo were busy!" De said, nodding his approval at his comrades' handiwork. The three walked into the submarine to find Rod at the controls and Mo silently leaning against a wall, near where he had frozen the android's other hand over the hole in the hull.

"Next stop, the factory," Rod said uncharacteristically quietly. As he took the sub back underwater, Don looked at Mo and noticed his expression. He asked him what was the matter, but his friend refused to answer, and just kept staring at Rod. M also tried to figure out what was wrong, but Rod wasn't talking either. He just drove the sub as quickly as he could to their destination.

The factory was in a smooth underwater grotto. The building itself was settled near the stone back "wall" of the area and away from the water. Several other submarines were lined on the outside, no doubt used to transport new androids to the surface. The factory itself was just as expansive as the unfinished one in Rumas, with even more androids hanging around the outside of it.

"Alright guys, this is the real deal: a fully functioning factory that we have to bring down. You guys ready?" asked De. After everyone responded in their own way, he continued. "Well, let's go!"

De charged out of the sub, with M in tow. The two immediately engaged the androids outside of the factory. Don, holding a map of the factory in one hand and his stun gun from the prison in the other, followed and joined the fray. Mo went after him but was stopped by Rod. Mo flinched when Rod's hand touched him.

"What? The others are fighting, we should help."

"In a minute. Look, I don't take back what I said, I still think you're weak-" Rod began.

"And I still think you're a petty criminal," Mo interrupted.

Rod let that slide. "But, for the sake of getting this over with, we should forget about...everything else that was said in here and call a truce," he let Mo go and stuck out his hand.

Mo turned around and glanced at Rod's hand for a

second.

"I didn't say anything that I'm ashamed of," he said uneasily.

"Look come on man," Rod was genuinely trying to appease his fellow Elemental, and in his mind Mo was unwilling to compromise. "Can't we just...you know, not talk about that anymore?"

"Fine. Until my Dad is out of jail and you're in, where you belong, we're in a truce," he said, finally taking Rod's hand.

Rod chuckled and squeezed Mo's hand tightly, making him wince. "Stronger and better men than you have tried to lock me up," he released Mo's hand and ran outside.

Mo stared after him and fought back the angry tears in his eyes. "I hate him..." he growled and exited the ship as well.

Fun Times in the Factory

By the time Rod and Mo made it outside the sub, the others were already inside the factory fighting (and losing) to about a dozen androids. The two late arrivals looked for a way to help their comrades, and Rod looked back towards the water outside.

"Open the doors!" He barked at Mo, who reluctantly obliged. Rod focused his power and brought a huge wave of the water through the doors that washed over the battling Elementals and androids.

"Hey!" De yelled; the flame he was about to throw had been doused.

"You could've warned us!" Don gurgled through a mouthful of water. The androids had already begun to recover from the water attack.

"Then they would've known the plan," Rod explained. "M, now!"

M used a great bit of his energy to send a wave of electricity over the androids, causing them to short out. He collapsed on the floor with the androids.

"How...did...you know...that would work?" he breathed.

"I didn't, now let's get started before it stops working!" Rod answered.

De opened the door to the spare parts room and called to the people he had told to hide inside. "You can come out now. Get out of here, grab a sub and go home," he told the large man in the front of the group.

"Thank you, thank you so much! My name is Darryl Fienburg, I'm the mayor of Rivera, please come see me when you're done!" he shook De's hand, bowed to the others and led the group out of the factory. Moments later, they heard a sub start up and head for the surface.

"Well, what do we do first Don?" Mo asked.

"I wish I knew, but Rod's bright idea soaked my map!" Don complained, shaking the wet map in their faces. Rod looked unapologetic.

"How are we supposed to know how to bring this place down then? It's not half-finished like the other one, we'll need actual weak spots to hit," M looked at the other four, hoping for an answer.

De had one. "We wing it! Two of you head to the top floor and start tearing this place up!" he yelled, starting to shoot fire at the walls.

"That makes no...whatever," M said, but followed De's order and headed to the top floor with Mo. They were stopped on the stairs by a group of androids, clearly not happy with them being there.

"Elemental Traitors! Cease this rebellious activity at once!" they chanted. M quickly silenced the one in front with an electric blast, and his nine comrades attacked the others. De took a deep breath and blew fire at the androids coming for him. The heat slowed them down, but didn't stop them. The androids retaliated with a few laser blasts that the rest of the team had to evade. De stopped his fire breathing when one blast nicked his shoulder and ducked behind a huge pile of defective parts with the others.

"You think they'll fall for the same trick twice?" M asked Rod over the sound of the blasts.

"I can't bring any water in with the doors closed, I need some more in here," he answered, moving away from the toppling android parts. Their makeshift cover wouldn't last much longer.

"Use the coolant!" Don yelled suddenly. The others stared at him. "All of these factories have cooling tanks in case they overheat, I remember seeing them on the plans, and this one's should be...there!" he pointed at a large tank in the far corner of the huge room.

"Got it, cover me!" Rod ran from their shelter, and the other Elementals came out fighting. M and De were shooting their respective elements at the androids to take their attention away from Rod, and Mo and Don helped by throwing the spare parts at them. Rod kept running, dodging both lasers and De and M's counterattacks until he was right in front of the tank. He stretched his hand to it, sensing the liquid inside the tank. He closed his eyes and focused on the liquid, willing it to come rushing out of the tank and into the room. It worked eventually, and Rod sent gallons of yellow colored liquid gushing onto the floor of the room behind him. The force of the rushing coolant knocked everyone else in the room off of their feet, and Rod fell into the broken tank, ignoring the cuts it gave him. From inside of it he yelled to his comrades, "Try it M!"

The androids and the Elementals began to pull themselves off of the wet floor when M got an idea of his own.

"Get off the floor!" he yelled to his comrades. They ducked and dodged the androids' attacks and jumped up the stairs, taking care to keep their hands off the railing. The androids were in hot pursuit, splashing through the coolant after them.

"Oh no you don't," M sneered. He placed his hands on the floor, sending several charges through the water in the coolant, causing the androids to fizzle and the machines connected to the floor to short circuit and explode. M fell to the ground again as the others cheered for the Water and Electric Elementals' teamwork.

"Are you guys ok?" De asked, treading carefully back through the coolant and the broken machines.

"I don't know how many more times I can do that..." M admitted. He still laid on the ground, exhausted. Rod had gotten out of the tank and was slowly walking back towards them.

"You gone keep doing it as long as it keeps helping us win," Rod said breathlessly.

"I agree, but why don't you two take a breath outside for a second? That had to have taken a lot out of you guys," De said. Rod nodded and hoisted M up so they could walk outside. "Ok," he looked around the first floor at the broken machines and started thinking. Maybe they didn't need to destroy the building, just what was inside it..."Okay, new plan. Don, Mo, let's go to these upper floors and take out the machines up there." The remaining heroes nodded their agreement and followed De up the stairs.

The second floor of the factory seemed much smaller than the first, mostly because it had a lot more rooms. De peeked in the first room and figured it must be used for training, since it was mostly open with only a few broken targets littered around it. He closed the door and faced the other two. "Ok, I'm gonna start wrecking in here, can you guys find and take out the computers?"

Don and Mo nodded. "Let's try that room over there!" Don suggested, and the two took off to a room further down the hall from the training room. De opened the door to the training room again and lit a flame so he could see. He noticed that there were three targets still intact at various points along the wall of the far side of the room and decided to have a little fun. He aimed for the targets to see if he could hit them from where he stood, throwing fire at all three. He hit two but just nicked the third. He kept aiming for the third target but kept missing.

"I've gotta work on my aim..." De said to himself. He suddenly heard a whirring sound and the lights in the room switched on. "Guess they found the controls," he said, and decided to try to hit the target with the new light. After a couple tries, he finally hit it. "Yes!" he yelled, jumping up in triumph. "Ok, well that was fun, let me start-" He stopped suddenly, having heard what sounded like very large footsteps. Just as had begun thinking he imagined the sound, there was a tremendous crashing noise. He ran outside of the room and right into Don and Mo. "What happened?!" De yelled.

"I don't know! We had taken out one computer and went for the other one when some...THING came to life and attacked us!" Mo said. He looked positively terrified.

"What..." De began, but he was soon answered. There was another loud crash, and around the corner came a metal creature at least ten feet tall, looking for blood. It was a shiny silver color and vaguely humanoid in shape, but its face was far more stiff and inhuman than any android they had ever seen. Two large funnel-like jets stuck out of its back, and the thing had a sharp blade on one hand and the other hand had same laser firing orb as the androids. Its humungous feet rocked the floor with every step it took towards the heroes.

"RUN!!!" De screamed, racing down the stairs, with the others right on his heels. Unfortunately for them, the monstrosity of metal wasn't far behind either. It had swung at the heroes before they ran, and took a big chunk of the second floor corridor with it. Now as it came down the stairs they creaked and groaned under its weight.

No doubt hearing all the commotion inside, Rod and M ran back into the factory, but stopped at the door when they saw the thing. "What the hell is that?!" Rod stammered

"Just keep running!" Don yelled, shoving past them and out the door. The others ran outside as well when the stairs had obviously had enough and collapsed under the weight of the thing and they both went crashing to the ground, shaking the very foundation of the factory, knocking several pieces off it off. Once the dust settled the Elementals approached the building to see if it was over. The giant robot laid on its back in the rubble of the staircase inside.

"Is...is it dead?" M asked nervously. As an answer, the heroes heard what was unmistakably the sound of a small jet engine whirl to life and propel the thing towards them.

The Elementals and Don all screamed in pure horror as they scrambled to get away from the racing machine. M shot a large bolt of electricity over his shoulder to try to stop the thing, but it easily shrugged that off. It did seem to be irritated by M's attempt, and went after the smallest Elemental. M screamed again and ended up running into a corner as the thing closed in.

De focused as intently as he could on the flames coming from the thing's engine, and was able to make them larger. The added propulsion sent the machine careening into the wall where M was standing, and the Elemental ducked just in time for the thing to fly over him. The thing made a gaping hole in the wall, making the building rumble and shake again while M ran for his life back to the others.

"Any idea on how to stop this thing?!" he screamed.

"I don't think our trick is gonna work on it!" Even Rod was panicked, and for good reason.

"I think I have an idea-" Don started, but the whirring sound started up again, and the android blasted itself out of the rubble, sending debris all over the first floor, damaging the structure even more.

"This thing is gonna bury us in this place!" Mo yelled as the robot started walking towards them again.

Rod looked at the floor and noticed the water still there. He focused on it and moved his hand in a motion that made a miniature whirlpool under the robot's feet, making it hard for it to keep walking.

"Whatever your plan is, you might wanna start talking!" he yelled. Already the robot was fighting hard against his power.

Don started talking a mile a minute. "This thing was activated by Mo and I messing with the second computer upstairs, if I can get back up there and shut everything back down, it should stop the robot, but I need you guys to buy me some time to do it, plus I need a way up there," he pointed at the wrecked stairs.

The metal monster had outlasted Rod's focus and

powered through the mini whirlpool to keep walking towards them. It was now Mo's turn to try to stop the thing. He stepped forward and used the water still on the floor to freeze the ground below the robot. Apparently, it wasn't equipped for icy surfaces and went crashing to the floor, knocking some parts of the floor above them down on top of it and the heroes. They ducked and moved to avoid getting crushed under the falling roof, but not even that was enough to stop the giant robot for long. It had already started to pick itself up off of the floor by the time De turned to Don.

"Okay, we're gonna try your plan before there is no second floor for you to go to, come on!" De grabbed Don and they ran to where the stairs were, while the others continued to use their powers to try to keep the robot on the ground. As soon as De and Don reached the landing, De told Don to wrap his hands around his neck and hold on tight. He used his fire powers to propel the two of them onto the second floor. The fire needed to launch both of them upwards was so great that De collapsed as soon as Don was back on his own two feet.

"Are you ok?" Don asked

"I'm fine! Ju-just go!" De said to the floor, and Don ran off to the computer room.

On the first floor, the robot was done playing around and was now firing off its gigantic laser blasts at the Elementals. The trio downstairs was sure that if one of them got hit it would be over for them, so they did everything they could to make the thing hit the walls and not them. They had given up trying to fight the monstrosity and just allowed it to fire its blasts at the walls to keep it busy until Don had done what he needed to. Not even De above them was safe; as one blast came towards him he had to muster up enough energy to roll farther down the hallway to safety.

Inside the computer room, Don was waiting on his pocket device to finish uploading his patented kill program to the computer. "Come on, come on stupid thing!" he urged the computer. He could hear the commotion under him clearly; the Elementals were screaming and yelling as they started to run out of places to hide from the robot destroying the building around them. The building shook more and more violently every time the giant robot's laser attacks hit it, and Don was pretty sure in moments he would be under the remains of the third floor if he didn't hurry. When the program finally uploaded, Don began typing as fast as his fingers could move. He needed to make sure it would work, or none of them would survive much longer. After what seemed like the longest minute or two, Don was seconds from shutting the whole system down when he very faintly heard what sounded like someone yell, "DON WATCH OUT!" before one of the gigantic laser blasts burst upwards from the first floor. He was close enough to the attack that the heat from the blast made him sweat, but not be harmed. He lifted a shaking finger to press the ENTER button on his device, and watched as the blast quickly died down and the computer made a number of error message noises.

The building itself also seemed to have had enough. No doubt due to that last blast shooting straight upwards, the third floor started to cave in, and the other Elementals were now screaming for Don and De to get out. Don heaved himself back to what remained of the quickly collapsing second floor corridor and stooped down to help De off the ground. He carried (or dragged) De to the ledge where he saw a shaky looking ice ramp Mo and Rod had created for them.

"COME ON!" Mo shrieked from the bottom of the ramp. Don pushed De's barely conscious body down the ramp before sliding down it himself. Rod grabbed De and helped him out of the factory and the four of them reached the outside in just enough time to see the last of the Rivera factory fall onto itself.

"We did it…" Don said, falling the ground outside the factory.

"No, *you* did it." Mo clarified, taking the moment to hug his best friend tightly. Don looked at the other three, and even M had to nod his agreement with Mo's words. If Don hadn't proved his worth to the team any other time, he definitely had today.

Dictator in Distress

The room was pitch black. Del's eyes frantically searched the room for some source of light but found none. He didn't like being called into A.G.'s chambers like this, especially in total darkness.

"You have failed. Explain," from what seemed to be the center of the room two very small green lights appeared.

"I...I...forgive me, Queen..." Del stuttered. A.G.'s green eyes flashed brighter and shot a highly concentrated laser beam in his direction. Unlike the more wide blasts from the other android's, A.G.'s beams were piercing; had Del not teleported and reappeared in the center of the room the blast could have easily gone through his side, or worse.

"The Pru Empire does not forgive, nor do I. You have failed far too much, Delico. Your failure must be punished."

"No, no, I'll fix it! I promise, I promise!" Del pleaded as the eyes started to glow again. "Please O Powerful One, we still have three other factories! The Elementals won't infiltrate them, I assure you, not if you let me live!" he got on his knees where he was to show his sincerity.

As if to disprove this, there was a knock on the door. "Enter," A.G. said, and in stepped the Silver Man. The light of the outside showed A.G. only for a moment, sitting straight on the throne she stole from the Underground Kingdom with the Orange Scepter in her hands. She was clothed in the nearly sheer and quite ornate gown she had worn ever since she had stolen the Orange Scepter. Its black color contrasted almost beautifully with her pale white "skin" and blonde "hair."

Her face showed no expression, which only made the fear on both the Silver Man and Del's more pronounced. "For what reason are you here? Explain," A.G. said.

The Silver Man also got to his knees and bowed in the darkness. "Queen A.G., the Elemental prisoners have been moved to their final location. With your approval, they will be ready to serve you."

"Excellent. They will be valuable additions to the Pru Empire. How fitting for them. See to it that they are prepared to aid in the takeover," A.G. said, dismissing the Silver Man.

"Yes, my-" he began, but at that moment another person raced into the room. The door bursting open made Del and the Silver Man jump, but A.G. just stared at it.

"My Queen," the female android started. "We have just lost connection with the Rivera factory; we fear that it may have been... compromised."

A.G.'s voice neither rose nor fell, but remained the same monotone. "Who are you? Explain."

The female stuttered as she responded. "I-I am Android 3217, co-codenamed Megan, my Queen. I am one of the reconnaissance androids you have stationed in Rivera to learn more about how the humans live..."

"3217, you have interrupted my judgment and

abandoned your assigned task. You have left the city of Rivera, and you have allowed one of the factories to be infiltrated. Explain."

"I'm sorry, O Powerful One. I-it wasn't completely my fault, please have mercy, forgive me!" Megan begged. She bowed as well.

"The Pru Empire does not forgive, nor do I. You have failed far too much, 3217. Your failure must be punished." Instead of simply firing a blast from her eyes, A.G. aimed the Orange Scepter at the still pleading android.

The intensity of the lime green blast from the scepter lit up the room and raced past both Del and the Silver Man and towards the android bowing near the door. The force of it completely obliterated the android, reducing it to a few metal limbs in seconds. The Silver Man shook his head sadly, and Del whimpered quietly.

"Approach, both of you," A.G. said to the Silver Man and Del. The two moved from their hiding place away from the destruction and bowed at A.G.'s feet. "This resistance can be no more. You two must quell it in the name of the Pru Empire; protect the last two factories with your lives. I leave Rockdale and Greater Grandia to you two. Do not fail."

"Yes, my Queen," they both answered.

"The Pru Empire must be reestablished, but it will not come to pass unless these Elementals are apprehended. They cannot be allowed to continue to sully the Empire's return."

"Yes, my Queen," Del and the Silver Man repeated. A.G. moved in the darkness, and both of them tensed up, ready to run from the room if they caught any glimpse of the Orange Scepter, or A.G. herself, firing again.

Instead the android began to pace the floor around her

throne. The slow constant sound of her black heels on the metal floor echoed around the large room. "Have the Battle Robots been perfected?"

"Yes, my Queen. Before the Rivera factory was taken the construction was finished. They are being taken to the other factories as we speak," The Silver Man answered. He decided not to mention the fact that one of them had been left to protect the Rivera factory.

"Are the new androids finished?"

"Nearly my Queen. They should be available to the other factories very soon," Del said. He expected A.G. to be angry that it wasn't one hundred percent done, but she seemed to be alright with it.

"These will be essential for the continuation of the Pru Empire's resurgence. With the Great Lands, the Underground Kingdom, and Grandia under our control we will easily be able to overtake Phorbes. The Shadow Lands will not put up a fight, and with all of them we shall easily overtake the Sky Nation as well. Once Redd Continent is under the Pru Empire's control, we shall be able to move to the rest of this planet."

The android continued to pace the floor as she spoke. Though Del and the Silver Man stayed in the room, A.G. continued thinking out loud. "It is time for the Pru Empire to retake its rightful place in the world. The dream of Ron ad Carrie Prudence must be reborn, and for that to happen the Elemental Resistance must be quelled here. By any means...Bring the monk," she said to neither of them in particular. Del got up to leave, but the Silver Man was faster.

"Delico," she said.

Del shook with nervousness again while the Silver Man speed walked out of the room. "Yes my Queen?"

A.G. pointed the Orange Scepter at him, and Del gasped. "You will live only because you still have value. But be warned, the Pru Empire does not tolerate failure, nor do I. Complete this task or you shall lose far more than you already have."

Del swallowed. If he hadn't already known, he knew now which factory he would have to go to, he couldn't let A.G. attack his home again.

The Silver Man returned with a lanky monk, dressed from his chest to his large feet in a brown robe that matched his skin tone. His bald head shined in the light for only a moment before the door closed again. The Silver Man shoved the monk closer to A.G., and he stumbled and fell onto the floor. "Leave now, both of you." A.G. said.

"Yes my Queen," they said for the third time, and both of them left the room as quickly as they could.

A.G's eyes moved in the darkness as she looked at the monk. "You will tell me of the locations of the other three Mystic Items now. Speak."

The monk got up from the floor and looked directly at A.G. "I will do no such thing! I have taken an oath to protect the Mystic Items from people like you; it's bad enough you have the Orange Scepter, I won't help you get the others!" his deep voice trembled a bit, knowing that he was almost certainly signing his own death certificate.

"The Pru Empire must possess all the powers of this world in order to reestablish itself as the most powerful organization on the planet, and for that, it must have the strength of all four Mystic Items. Having any less is failure, and the Pru Empire does not tolerate failure, nor do I." Even when the machine was clearly angry her voice never changed its tone; making her anger that much more chilling.

The monk was shaken but would not be swayed. "Well you had better get used to it, because you will never have the other items!" Quietly, the monk began reciting his death rites.

A.G. sat back on her throne. She continued to stare at the monk, who was now full on praying. A.G.'s eyes began to glow their green color, and from them shot two very thin laser blasts.

The blasts were nowhere near as powerful as those from the Orange Scepter, but still more than powerful enough to puncture the monk's chest and kill him instantly. His body collapsed loudly onto the floor. One of the androids from outside A.G.'s chambers peeked in nervously.

"Remove him," A.G. said. The android nodded and heaved the monk out of the room, leaving the dictator alone in the darkness once again.

The Legend of the Orange Scepter

With the factory gone, the city of Rivera showered the Elementals and Don with praise. The Elementals were able to either destroy or chase out the androids still in the city and return Rivera to a level of peace and tranquility it hadn't had for almost four months.

"Don't these people know that A.G. could still send more androids here? Or that the rest of the country is still hers?" M wondered when yet another family tearfully thanked them.

"Let the people have their moment man," Rod replied.

De nodded his agreement. "They probably do realize it, but they're happy for right now, so leave them be," M shrugged and faked a smile for a picture with the family.

The heroes were given as many free nights as they wanted in the city's finest hotel (or at least the finest hotel the city had left). After their third night however, they decided it was time to move on. None of them really wanted to give up their luxury life, especially not Rod who felt they deserved it, or M who did not want to go back to "roughing it", but knowing that (with the help of a manic robot) they had destroyed another factory, the time was ripe for them to keep their good luck streak going.

However, they couldn't leave without talking to the mayor as he requested time and time again, so the next morning they went to pay him a visit. They took a boat ride the mayor's island just as he asked; hopefully he would be able to give them some useful information.

"Friends!" he beamed when he greeted them at the edge of the water. "Please, come, come!"

"Thank you so much, Mayor Fienburg," De said as they started walking to his house.

"Please, you are friends! Call me Darryl," Mayor Fienburg said, waving off all pleasantries.

"Ok Darryl, do you think you can tell us if you found out anything while you were in the factory? Anything at all that could help," Mo wasted no time. A few people who lived on the mayor's island waved from their balconies and patios at the heroes as they passed.

Mayor Fienburg's smile towards one group of onlookers faltered. "I can, but I'm afraid that you might not like what you will hear," he admitted.

"Please Darryl, whether we want to know or not, we have to know everything we can in order to bring A.G. down," Don pleaded. By this time they were inside his house and standing around in his living room. Mayor Feinburg's butler looked eagerly at the six of them, no doubt waiting on this news.

Mayor Fienburg sighed. "Alright, follow me," he led the boys to his library. The five sat (or in Rod's case, leaned) at various places around the room, and Mayor Fienburg himself sat behind his work desk. He looked at them all in turn before continuing.

"I was there for two months; I learned a lot. Do you

know where the other factories are?"

"There was one being built in Rumas, but we took that one out," M said.

"Plus the one we just wrecked here," Rod boasted.

"There's one in Greater Grandia," De added.

"And one in Rockdale" Don finished.

"Exactly. So you should know that the Rockdale factory is the closest, and that that's probably where you should go next," Mayor Fienburg said.

"Yeah, we have actually been to Rockdale already. It's strange though, there weren't really any androids there when we were there," Mo said.

"They don't need them there, most of the citizens in the Underground Kingdom serve A.G. willingly," Mayor Fienburg pointed out. All five boys looked at him in disbelief. He smiled sadly. "It's true, I assure you. No one knows why exactly. Some think it's because of what she did to their country, and it wasn't exactly a paradise in the first place, you know? I'm sure it has something to do with the fact that one of A.G.'s main henchmen is from there, though. I think his name was Kel, Bell, or something like that..."

"Del..." M realized. The others nodded.

"Rod, you're good at thinking like a criminal, why would Del or any of the people in the Underground Kingdom work for A.G. willingly?" Mo asked.

Rod narrowed his eyes, but answered anyway. "For power probably. The status maybe. Willingly working for her would let him get close enough to A.G. to get some perks."

Mayor Fienburg pondered this for a moment. "That actually fits. I remember when we first started working that huge Battle Robot thing-sorry about that by the way; they found out about the engineering college here they had the students building all kinds of stuff. But anyway, that Del fellow was one of the people there to see the thing. The head androids told him that he would get one for his factory once they perfected it. They said A.G. would get one too, not like she needs it as long as she has the Orange Scepter."

Mo, M, Don and Rod all exchanged looks. "So, it's true then? The rumors? She really does have the Orange Scepter? I know what the news stations said but I just never really believed..." Mo whispered. Mayor Fienburg didn't even look at him when he nodded.

"I saw it in her hands when she came to check the progress of the factory."

"What's the Orange Scepter?" De asked. Everyone stared at him.

"You don't know what the Orange Scepter is?!" M demanded. "Who taught you history?"

De laughed. "I'm self-taught. No school, remember?"

"The Orange Scepter-" Don began. He had to talk loudly to drown out M muttering about how "an idiot was going to lead them to their doom" "-is the national treasure of Redd Continent, the continent we live on. After the villain Childress nearly took over the world, the Mystics blessed each of the four continents with a powerful item that, should something like that happen again, a generation of Elementals could use the four items to fight the threat off."

"Only now, apparently, it's gonna be used *against* the Elementals," Rod added.

"What does it do?" De asked.

Mayor Fienburg answered this time. He pulled out a book from the shelf nearest him and flipped a couple pages.

"'The Orange Scepter has the ability to amplify the natural abilities of any whom wield it. It was created for the specific purpose of strengthening Elemental and Elemental-like powers.'" He closed the book and looked up at the heroes surrounding him.

"But since she has it, she uses it to amp up her own powers. You know those lasers that most of the androids have? Well, that place where the factory was had a mountain there when A.G. first got here. When she left there wasn't a mountain anymore."

"Oh wow..." De said. He remembered the smooth, clear area of the underwater grotto.

"Exactly. With the Orange Scepter, A.G. can't be beat. For you guys to have any chance against her, you will have to take it away from her. And that's not even the worst part," Mayor Fienburg told them.

"Oh, there's more good news?" M muttered.

Mayor Fienburg kept talking anyway. "Now that you guys have taken down the factory here, A.G. is going to no doubt tighten security. She could be waiting for you in Grandia or Rockdale herself. Would you guys be able to handle that?" The heroes looked at one another. "There's nothing wrong with stepping away, you're only kids after all."

For the first time since the journey started, someone made reference to the Elementals' age. While all of them were still in their early teens, they felt that had done more than enough to prove their worth, and detested being looked down on because of their ages. They had all decided once the Racksons were taken that they were in this for the long haul. Truthfully, it had probably happened back when they met the orphaned store owner in Rockdale, but either way, they refused to be deterred in their mission. Whether Mayor Fienburg realized it or not, his comment solidified them leaving, rather than the opposite.

"We can handle whatever she throws at us," De said, while the others nodded. "We appreciate your concern Mayor Fienburg (everyone, including Mayor Fienburg, noticed the renewed formalities), but if we don't take A.G. down no one will. We are the last hope. No one's gonna try it after us, so we have to try as hard as we can."

"You boys are either very, very brave or very, very stupid..." Mayor Fienburg said after a moment.

"And sometimes both..." Rod muttered. Don nudged him.

"If you really plan on taking down the other two factories you will need all the rest and supplies you can get. Please, stay here one last night, and allow me to help you get to Rockdale in the morning," Mayor Fienburg offered.

"We would greatly appreciate that, but...how..." M began.

Mayor Fienburg smiled again. "Oh don't worry about how, I have a plan..."

"I have a delivery of some spare parts from Grandia," Mayor Fienburg told the androids outside the shipment truck.

"Fine delivery civilian. Take it to the back," replied the android standing at the gate. The guard android looked suspiciously at the android in the truck beside Mayor Fienburg, but thankfully Don had been able to make "Larry" look very much like he was still activated. When Mayor Fienburg reached the back of the factory, he opened the back of the large truck and wheeled five large boxes into the factory's back door.

"Good luck boys," Mayor Fienburg whispered, as he got back in the truck and headed back to Rivera.

Four of the five boxes began to shake violently after a few minutes, and the four Elementals broke out of them.

"I can't believe that actually worked," Mo commented. He helped Don to break out of his box while the others surveyed where they were.

"Mayor Fienburg was a little rough with my box..." M complained, rubbing his tail bone.

"At least he did what he did for us," De said. "Everybody ready?"

"Give me a stun gun Don." Don grabbed one out of his bag and handed it to Mo.

"Here's hoping there's not another one of those robot things in here..." M said with a shudder.

"Whatever's in here, it's gonna get taken down with the rest of this place. Let's get started," De kicked open the doors from the supply room and entered the main part of the factory, which, for once, was completely empty.

"Where is everybody?" Mo asked. The lack of people or androids on the first floor made them all a little nervous, all but one.

"Who cares? Let's just wreck this place and leave," Rod suggested. He walked towards the coolant tank to get some water into the building, but was very quickly cut off by Del teleporting in front of him. Rod had just enough time to see Del wearing a black coat with fur on the collar, a black almost skintight shirt and a pair of tight fitting blue jeans before the villain punched him in the face. Rod stumbled and swung at the air when Del disappeared again. He reappeared behind the other heroes and kicked Don in the back. Don fell to his knees, but before anyone could retaliate he was gone again.

M looked around frantically for the teleporter when he reappeared in front of him, hand outstretched to use his energy blast on the Elemental. M's reflexes kicked in and he grabbed Del's hand. The blast was redirected upstairs, blowing straight through a part of the factory. Both were surprised for a fraction of a second, before M shocked Del with his electricity. The electrocution stopped Del just long enough for Rod to send some of the coolant tank's water rushing towards him. Mo started freezing the water around Del, but the crafty warrior disappeared once again.

"I really wish he would stay in one place..." De muttered. The five stood back to back in the middle of the abandoned factory searching every corner for the trademark green flash.

Instead, the doors to the factory burst open, and Del stood in them flanked by ten androids. His expression was strange when he finally addressed the Elementals. "You five have caused a lot of trouble, you know."

"Yeah, for you!" Mo piped in.

"Yes, for me! How dare you come here, to my home-don't you know what's at stake? Don't you understand-?"

"All we need to understand is that you're on the wrong side, buddy, and you've gotta go down," M cut him off.

"Stupid little...fine. FINE! You'll see. I'll make you see!" Del roared, and he and the ten androids attacked the Elementals.

Rod ran back to the coolant tank and stretched out his hands. He had noticed before that there was a lot less liquid in there than there was in Rivera, so he had to send the last of it rushing towards Del and the androids. As soon as the androids were sufficiently soaked, M began shooting electricity at them in hopes of short circuiting them. When his targets didn't fizzle and spark, Del started to laugh.

"Did you really think that Queen A.G. wouldn't have figured out your little tricks by now? These androids have a rubber lining under their outer layer, you can't short circuit them!"

Mo and Don tossed away their stun guns, realizing that they too, would be useless against these new androids. They all had to duck behind the assembly line, since the androids' laser attacks worked just as well as ever.

"What are we going to do?!" Mo panicked.

"Get killed if we don't think of something quick!" Rod answered. He looked towards their leader "De, what-"

"I have an idea!" M announced. "Don, do you remember if the main fuse box is on this floor?"

Don reached into his bag and pulled out a map as De and Rod kept pelting their attackers. "If each factory is built the same, the main power should be right about...there!" he pointed to the far corner of the room, where they all saw a small black box connected to the wall.

"Works for me!" M said. He ran from his shelter and towards the fuse box, utilizing his small size to dodge lasers as he ran. De and Rod leapt from their shelter as well to try and keep him from getting blown up by the androids by hitting them with as much as they could muster. M flung the fuse box open and placed his hands inside. He focused all of the electrical energy he had into overloading the power. Lights shone brilliantly bright, the conveyer belt started moving insanely fast, and they heard the computers upstairs power up at full volume. A few seconds later, the electronics in the building all began to explode from their power surge. The conveyer belt ran off track and lights all over the floors broke, sending a flurry of sparks dancing onto the floor. Some of them touched the flames De had been flinging, and in moments fire was everywhere.

"What did you just do?!" Rod yelled. One of the sparks had just missed him when he ran over to M. The youngest Elemental, however, had fallen to the ground. He spoke, barely audible.

"If...if I can't beat...these guys...we can...we can at least...bring this place down..." The energy required to overload such a large system had taken a lot out of him, and his exhaustion won out as he lost consciousness.

Del, who had been fighting Mo hand to hand, noticed the now burning building. "What is going..." he looked to the others and watched De use the new flames to keep the androids at bay. As De started throwing flames at one android in particular, Del noticed that one of the flying embers went through a hole in the wall and ignited something outside of the factory. "Oh no no no!" he called. He teleported from his battle with Mo and towards the flame thrower. "You're coming with me," he spat, grabbing De and teleporting them both out of the building.

"Where...where did they go?" Mo wondered aloud.

Del had taken De to what looked to be a playground in a housing complex, judging the equipment and the many apartments around them. De threw Del off him and launched a few flames his way. One of them caught Del's foot as he jumped out of the way. One, however, missed Del completely and hit a nearby apartment building, setting it ablaze almost instantly.

"No!" De said. He stretched his hand out to try to shrink the flame, but a fair amount of damage was already done. Del had moved to the top of the jungle gym and he watched De lament over what he had done.

"Watch what you're doing!" Del screamed. "Are you trying to burn down the city? Be careful!" De shot another flame at him, both in anger at Del and at his mistake, but thankfully it was aimed high enough that when Del teleported away it didn't hit any more apartments.

Del reappeared behind De, and though he was physically smaller than the Elemental he was able to grab his arms and hold him for a second. "Now listen to me De, I have something you might want to know, a couple things, actually..." he whispered to him.

Apparently De wasn't in the listening mood. "The only thing I want to know is that you and all your androids are dead!" he snapped. He kicked back in Del's shins to get him off of him. Del yelped in pain and hopped backwards, holding his leg. He shot an energy blast towards De, but could only look in horror as De leapt out of the way and the blast hit another one of the apartments. There was a gaping hole where the attack hit, but as far as the two could see no one was inside.

De chuckled. "Looks like you have to be careful too...wouldn't want to hurt any of *your* people!"

Del was shaking with rage. He ran towards the Fire Elemental with a renewed purpose. "Fine! If you won't listen, I'll make you hear me!"

"WAKE UP!" Rod screamed, yanking M off the ground and trying to shake him back to consciousness. "These guys are gonna make sure we all burn in here!" he looked around frantically for any remaining water on the ground, but Mo was using it to maintain a constantly melting ice shield around them as they came up with a plan. The sound of the androids' lasers hitting Mo's shield rang in their ears.

"I have another idea, but it's a long shot," Don looked up from his map to interrupt.

"Whatever it is, do it!" Rod barked.

"Aye aye, captain! Be right back!" Don ducked around the waning ice barrier and moved as quickly as he could to the parts room, taking care not to get blasted as he ran.

"I'll never understand these people..." Rod complained. He looked on the ground and noticed a few melted ice puddles that Mo wasn't using, so he dropped M and helped Mo hold the androids back.

Out of fear of missing and damaging more homes, De and Del had resorted to fist fighting. Besides the occasional teleportation from Del, both boys had resigned themselves to not use their powers. The two's "street fight" had actually attracted spectators from the neighborhood, all wide eyed at the brawl right outside their homes. It was clear from their cheers who the Rockdale citizens wanted to win.

"Show him what we're made of!" an older gentleman chanted from the fence around the playground. Del looked up after he gave De a particularly strong kick and smiled at him. This gave De just enough time to jump on Del's back. Since De was larger than Del, his weight forced Del to the ground and unable to move. The crowd began to boo De, and a couple boys around the two fighters' age actually moved forward like they were going to help Del. De raised his hand and created a line of fire in front of them that sent them all scattering. Del tried to get up, but De forced his head into the ground.

"Are you going to kill me in front of my people?" Del asked through a mouthful of dirt.

"Give me one reason why I shouldn't..." De replied. Deep within him though, he knew this was a bluff. Judging by his response, Del did too.

"Because you won't. And that's why you won't beat A.G. You have to be willing to do what you have to do," Del said back. De pushed his head deeper into the ground.

"You don't know what I have had to do, what we have had to do! We'll beat her and you, you'll see..." De's tone didn't even convince him.

"You don't know what I've had to do either," Del said solemnly, but his tone changed quickly while he had De distracted. "Let's see how your friends are doing, shall we?" Del said, and the two vanished. They reappeared on the factory floor, dangerously close to quite a few flames. De leapt off of Del and the two examined their surroundings.

Only Mo was still on the first floor holding what was unmistakably one of the androids' laser blasting hands. With a portable charger that no doubt came from Don, he had been able to take out all but two of the androids, as well as cause even more damage to the factory itself. Don walked quickly from upstairs with Rod in tow. M's still unconscious body was draped over Rod's shoulder, but judging by the explosions and dangerous rattling from above them, the two had still been able to cause some major damage to the upper two floors.

Del yelled and launched another energy attack at the Elementals nearest him, but both of them saw it and ran out of the way. The attack hit the doors to the factory and blew them open, giving them all a chance to escape the still burning building.

"De, come on!" Rod yelled as he left the building. The others weren't far behind him. With one final blast Mo shot at the last two androids full on, blowing them to pieces. De hit Del with one last blaze to distract him before he followed his comrades. Del jumped backwards and tripped over some debris, hitting his head and landing him, seemingly unconscious, on the floor with the pieces of the last two androids in the factory as it continued to burn.

"Whoo! Nice work guys!" De said once they were all outside. The outskirts of Rockdale even looked a little brighter because of their success.

"That's another factory down," Rod breathed. He gently laid M on the ground beside him. "Anybody got something that can wake up Sparky?"

"No, let him rest. He did good in there," De said.

"Yea, thanks to him and you we're almost done!" Don cheered. He placed Mo's laser hand in his bag for safe keeping, since Mo was likely to blow his leg off with it in his pocket.

"And one step closer to freeing my Dad!" Mo added. He and Don looked at each other and erupted into a bizarre sort of victory dance that no doubt came from one of the many adventure shows they watched. Rod and De shook their heads.

"Should we go get Del outta there? Or at least put the flames out?" Rod whispered to De.

De shook his head. "He can teleport. If he wants to live he can save himself. As for this place, it's not by anyone's house or anything, so I say let it burn to the ground. What I am worried about," De turned to Rod. "Is that you're getting soft dude. Is this the feared leader of the Heat Boyz I hear worried about somebody else's life?"

"Nah man! I just don't want us to end up as killers. You know, he is still a person, even if he's a-" Del himself appeared behind Rod and yanked him by the waist before vanishing again.

"What the...?" De yelled. The others stopped celebrating and could only watch as Del returned and teleported him off as well.

Poof. M was gone.

Poof. Mo.

Don shook as he looked around, utterly terrified, for the teleporter. He snatched the laser hand back out of his bag and turned from side to side, waiting for him to reappear. When Del did and reached a debris covered hand towards Don, he screamed and fired the laser hand at Del, sending him rolling across the ground, still smoking both from the blast and De's last fire attack. Don waited for Del to move again, but when he didn't, it began to settle in his mind that he was now alone with only Del's possibly no longer living body.

Divided

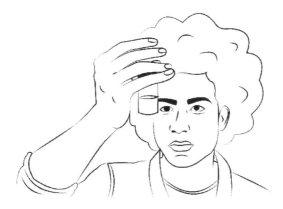

Don didn't know quite how to feel. On the one hand, it seemed like Del was finally beat, but he was now alone in Rockdale with no way of knowing where the others were. Where had Del taken them? How would they all find each other again? They still had one factory to destroy and an evil android dictator to take down, they couldn't afford this type of setback! Don's thoughts were interrupted when he heard people approaching. He turned around and saw a crowd of Rockdale's citizens around him.

"Oh...hello," Don said nervously. A few people in the crowd were pointing at him and Del and whispering.

"What have you done?" a man at the front of the crowd demanded.

Don jumped. "We...uh, destroyed the factory," he said, gesturing towards the still burning building behind him.

"No, not that, what have *you* done to our prince?" he pointed at Del's body.

"Pr-prince?" Shocked was an understatement. "Del's a prince?" Don asked, also looking back at the body.

"Yes! Our prince gave himself to A.G. to protect us, to

save us from her wrath! He was our only hope and you killed him! You've killed us all!"

"Without the factory and Prince Del, what will happen to our land?" an older woman in the crowd looked on the verge of tears as she spoke.

Don looked around at the crowd. Some smaller children were crying, and several of the adults were making threatening gestures towards him. He decided to try to diffuse the situation.

"Please, I assure you that the Elementals and I are well on our way to making sure that your land and the rest of the world is safe from A.G.," he swallowed hard. "I'm very sorry about your prince, but you will all-"

"What Elementals? All I see is you!" a boy about Don's age yelled from the crowd. Don began backing away from them.

"Exactly!" the man in the front agreed. "You're probably making all of this up, you work for A.G. don't you?"

"No, no!" Don said "I'm just saying-"

"I bet A.G. went back on her word and sent him here to kill the prince! She's gonna make our land her new headquarters! We'll all be slaves!" another voice from the crowd yelled.

"No, I have nothing to do with A.G., I promise!" Don yelled, still backing away from them. He was nearly back in the factory now.

"Well why do you have one of the android's lasers then? Liar!" another voice screamed. Don stuffed the laser hand in his bag.

"You're nothing but a liar!"

"He's gonna kill us all!"

"Just like he did our prince!"

"GET HIM!" the man in the front led the charge and the crowd rushed towards Don. Having a bit of a head start, Don raced around the back of the factory and through the back streets of Rockdale as fast as his legs could carry him. Finding and saving the Elementals from whatever Del put them through would have to wait, first he would have to save himself…

***

Rod spun around and swung at the air. He cursed when he realized that Del was long gone, and wondered where he had ended up.

Rod looked around; he was apparently in some type of city, but it was unlike any he had ever been before. He saw a lot of run down looking buildings with so much graffiti on the sides of them that he thought it was a new paint color, and a shady group of kids gambling down an alley not far from him. The roads looked ragged and full of potholes and he had appeared beside a building that he was sure had been used as a bathroom not long ago. What was most curious, however, was the fact that though he was certain it was still day time, the sky here was dark as if something was blocking the sun. It took him a moment to realize that this meant he must be in the Shadow Lands: the country on Redd Continent that was perpetually darkened because it sat under the shade of the floating country, the Sky Nation.

"The Shadow Lands ain't too bad. I thought it would be a lot worse," Rod grinned. He walked to the kids and they all looked up at him as he approached.

"What the hell you want?" one of them asked. Judging by the tooth he was missing he couldn't be any older than about ten.

"I want in," Rod said simply.

"No way! We don't even know you!" said another kid. His pasty skin and red hair made him look like a mix between Mo and De.

"Why should we let you in on this?" asked the only girl among them. Her many pigtails were missing several hair bows. Rod reached into his pockets and pulled out forty Redd Tokens.

"Whooaaa!" the three kids said in unison.

"That's a lot of money!" the second boy said. He had only five tokens in his hands.

"Ok you can play," the first kid relented and gestured for Rod to sit down.

"The game is called 'No Dice'! You have to make the dice land on or get close to a number you guess. If they land on a number we say, we get the money, if they land the number you say you get it. You got it?" Rod nodded. "Ok! Oh, and you gotta put in all your money!" the first kid looked at the other two and they smiled. "Do it!"

Rod could tell he was being hustled, but he noticed a doggie bowl full of water beside the kids and decided to go along with it. He may even have some fun with them afterwards. He nodded again and dropped his tokens on the ground with the others. The first kid, who seemed to be the leader, handed him the dice.

"Seven!" He smiled, showing his missing teeth as he said it.

"Twelve!" said the girl.

"Three," the other boy said.

"Umm, nine?" Rod guessed and tossed the dice. They landed on eight.

"Ha ha! I win! I get all the money," the "leader" reached

for Rod's tokens when he grabbed his hand.

"What? How?"

"You went over!" the leader explained. He tried to wiggle out of Rod's grip.

"You ain't say all that, you said it had to land on one of your numbers," Rod pointed out. The kid snatched his hand from him.

"Shut up dude! We won, just give us the money! Or..." he looked towards the other boy, who pulled a bat from the ground behind him. The girl looked menacingly at Rod, who just laughed. He looked back at the doggie bowl and gently splashed the three with some water from it. They all screamed and tried to run, but Rod reached out and grabbed the group's leader before he got far.

"Let me go dude! You can keep your money, alright! Let me go! Go on, let me go before I go get my Dad! He used to work for the Pru Empire, you know, he'll beat you up!" the kid threatened.

The words 'Pru Empire' reminded Rod of something he had heard Master Rackson tell them about A.G. "Your Dad worked for the Pru Empire? Like from thirty years ago? The one A.G. is screaming about nowadays?"

The kid continued to struggle against Rod's grip, so he splashed him some more to make him stop. Once the kid stopped squirming Rod set him down. Surprisingly, he didn't run. "Yeah. What of it?"

Rod stooped down but kept his eyes locked with the kid's. He couldn't help but see traces of himself in the boy's narrowed eyes. "You're gonna take me to meet your Dad. Now."

***

"We have already told the Android Goddess and her accomplices everything we know," the tiny monk was on his knees in the sand of the desert, pleading for mercy from the huge android that stood over him. "Please! Leave me alone."

"Speak the truth, Monk Civilian!" the android snapped. This android looked much taller than the others and had to stoop down to lift the monk's head. "Queen A.G. requires more power, how do you unlock the true potential of it?"

"It IS at its true potential! The Orange Scepter isn't all powerful...please, I told those two that last time they and A.G. were-"

"You will refer to her as Queen A.G.!" the android shoved the monk backwards. "And Queen A.G. serves the Pru Empire of her own accord, Masters Samantha and Kevon have gone back into hiding, and you will now tell Queen A.G. how to be all powerful, or perish...." the android leveled his laser hand at the pale, whimpering monk, ready to blow the man's bald head clean off his shoulders.

De finally stepped from behind the large boulder formation he had been crouched behind. The sudden appearance of a nearly six-foot brown skinned teen with red hair no doubt surprised both the monk and the android.

"Please help me!" the monk begged.

"Stand down civilian! This does not concern you!" the android turned back to the monk just as De launched an attack at his head.

"Actually, it does," De said, prepping another fire attack.

"Elemental Resistance!" the android snarled. He rushed towards De, shooting lasers as he ran. De ducked back behind his rocks and realized that this hadn't been his smartest idea. Just as he started to wonder how he would stop the android, the creation itself was standing over him.

"Oh...um. Hi..." De said. The android lifted De off the ground and because of its size was able to hold him in the air. De's arms were pinned by his sides by the android's grip, and his feet dangled in the air.

"You will face punishment from Queen A.G., Elemental. Prepare to be captured!"

"That already happened, but it's not happening again," De said. He took a deep breath and blew, covering the android's head in flames. The heat distracted the android just long enough for him to drop De. De started running towards the monk still standing frozen in fear the moment his feet touched the ground.

"What are doing still standing here?! Why didn't you run away?" De asked as he pelted the still recovering giant android with flames.

"I wanted to see him go down," the monk explained.

"Well that might not happen, so run already!" De said back. He kept hitting the android with all he had to stop it from overtaking them.

"If you can't defeat him, we have to get back to the Shrine where it's safe!" the monk continued, still not having moved.

Eventually De's fires had succeeded in shutting off the android, and it stopped rushing towards the two. De turned back to the monk. "No need. But you should've ran when I told you to, it could have gotten dangerous. Who are you anyway?" De asked.

"I am Nustaf, one of the monks from the Shrine of Kashiro, thank you so much Elemental!" Nustaf grabbed De's hand and shook it excitedly.

"Shrine of what?" De's lack of knowledge about Colorius lore was once again showing.

"The Shrine of Kashiro! It is the place where the Orange Scepter is usually held! We know the secrets of the Orange Scepter and guard it from potential thieves. In fact, I have some information that may be useful for you back at the Shrine," Nustaf explained. He grabbed De's hand and began leading him across the desert towards the shrine he called his home.

***

M slumped against the side of the nearest house. He had been walking for at least two hours since he woke up; aside from realizing he was in a town called Dayham and that he was close to the border between the Great Lands and Grandia, he had no clue what was going on. Where was Del? Why had he brought him here? Where were the others? They would have to get back together soon, it was the only way they would be able to take down the last factory and beat A.G. It would take all of their powers and skills to do it: Rod, Mo, Don, and De...

Hearing the name in his head made him angry all over again. How could he come in, literally fresh off the streets, and take his title away from him? He deserved to be the leader, after all he was the first Elemental and he was the one learning history before he even got his powers. He deserved it; he put in all the hard work, so why didn't he get the results? That is how it's supposed to be; it's what his parents always told him. You work hard, stay out of trouble, and good things will happen to you. Why did the gangster, the two nerds and the orphan off the street get more results than he did? Yeah, he had messed up a few times before, but everyone makes mistakes. He had to have made up for it now, after all, he was the one who was taking out androids left and right, and he was the one who really took out this last factory, so where was his reward? Hadn't he earned it? Wasn't he good enough to get one?

"Aren't I better than De?" M asked out loud.

"Who's there?" An older gentleman came around the corner of the house and peeked at M. He was wearing a too large house coat and pushed his glasses onto his peach colored face as he looked down the side of his home. M sighed and got up to leave.

"I'm sorry, sir. I didn't mean to disturb your home. I should be going anyway," M said.

"No, wait. You look like you have been on the move for a while. Wouldn't you care for a hot meal before you leave again?" the house's owner asked.

M's stomach growled at the prospect of food. It was about dinner time. "Sure. Couldn't hurt."

M followed the man into his house and to the kitchen at the back of it. The man brought M something that looked like pork and a rock hard roll, but he was too hungry to argue. He wolfed down the meat, but sensed his rudeness as the man stared at him.

"I'm sorry. I'm in your home, eating your food and I haven't even introduced myself. My name is Maurice Black, but most people call me M," he said, stretching his hand out.

"I guess I'm just as much to blame. I'm Gary Layto. I'm a scientist here in Dayham," Layto grabbed M's hand, and gave as firm a handshake as his age would allow. M went back to eating, but Layto apparently still had questions. "Well, as long as we are being slightly rude, may I ask you who 'De' is?"

M swallowed hard. "He's the guy who stole the title of Elemental generation leader from me," he said bitterly. Layto's jaw dropped.

"Elemental? You're an Elemental? Like, with the powers and everything?" Layto asked.

"Is there any other kind?" M laughed. "You're looking at the newest Electric Elemental," he boasted. He rubbed his hands together and showed Layto as his hands sparked with electricity. The old professor leapt up from the table in happiness and his chair loudly hit the ground.

"This is amazing!" Layto said. He started talking excitedly as he stared at M. "I've been studying Elementals and their powers for many years now. Some of my cohort and I even came up with a way to transfer Elemental-like powers to individuals without them through a mixture of science and magic known as the Power Blood transfer. I have been able to transfer Elemental-like powers to quite a few people, but with a real Elemental I could finally crack the code of giving full powers to other people! Please, let me get a sample of your blood, please!" Layto begged. M looked at him with both shock and disgust.

"Umm, thanks for the food, but I don't think I wanna be a blood donor. I think I had better be going now," M said. He got up and crept towards the door and turned around to open it. It was locked but he kept shaking the handle.

"But, Mr. M, if my experiment is successful I could give you extra powers just as I have given others. You could become the first Elemental of two different elements! That would surely make you better than this De you despise, wouldn't it?" Layto offered.

M stopped moving the door handle. If he was stronger the others would have no choice but to accept him as leader. The first two element Elemental...he could probably defeat A.G.

by himself then; Orange Scepter or no Orange Scepter. All of his hard work would finally pay off. Future generations would study *him* in their history. He would be a legend; way better than De or anyone else.

"Let's do it," M agreed. Layto clapped his hands together and ran to pick up his phone. M sat back down just in time to hear Layto say to the person on the other end "Get here, now!" and hang up. He beamed at M and showed him the way to his laboratory.

About fifteen minutes later M sat down on the cold operating table in Layto's lab. The room was in the basement of Layto's house; the drafty stone walled room was filled with machines, tools and books on various subjects. He looked around the room at the same time the boy who Layto had called sat down on the opposite side of the room. He looked to be maybe a year older than M, and the two actually favored one another, right down to the skin tone and tall afro. The only difference was he was a little taller than the miniscule Elemental.

"I'm being rude again, Mr. M! This is Lamont Vike. He is one of the people I told you about. I have already given him some abilities from another's blood I borrowed-"

"Borrowed? How do you 'borrow' blood?" M interrupted. "And why are you doing this anyway?"

"So many questions Mr. M! The Power Blood spell is a very curious phenomenon; many want to learn more about it and will do whatever it takes to do so. It is thanks to these generous donors that I am able to help people like you and Mr. Vike here." He picked up a notebook off a nearby shelf and began flipping pages. "Did you know that nearly every inhuman power is tied to that individual's blood? It is how people are able to pass certain abilities on to their children! Oh, I can't wait! With your Elemental blood I would be able to learn even more about the spell!" Layto looked positively giddy at the idea, but M still looked apprehensive. "I should then be able to give you his powers and make you stronger as well," added Layto.

M sighed and stuck out his arm. "Okay...do it..." he closed his eyes as he allowed Layto to draw his blood. He only winced slightly as the needle stuck him. "What sort of powers do you have?" he asked Lamont.

"Dark magic," he replied. His voice was gravely and serious.

M turned back to Layto. "I don't want dark powers. I was thinking you could give me like Psy powers, or Light, you know? Light and lightning...that would be cool."

"Nonsense Mr. M! You'll learn to love Dark Magic, just like Mr. Vike has, haven't you Mr. Vike?" Layto then moved to extract blood from Lamont.

"Yeah, it's cool, I guess," Lamont didn't flinch when Layto stuck him. Layto nodded, not looking at either boy as he worked. He held the two vials in his hands and began chanting incantations over them.

"Are you cursing my blood?!" M said in alarm.

Layto laughed when he finished. "No, no Mr. M! This isn't a curse; it's just part of the experiment. I told you it's a mix of magic and science that has to be done to give you his powers and vice versa. Now here, the two of you drink this and you should have each other's powers now," Layto handed each boy the vial of the other's blood, and to M's surprise Lamont actually drank his. There was a sound like the crackle of electricity, and Lamont passed out on the table. M yelled out.

"What happened to him?!"

"You are far too jumpy, Mr. M! This is all part of the transfer, now go ahead, and drink up."

M continued to stare at the vial in his hand and the unconscious boy on the other table. "You know what, Layto, I appreciate it, but no thanks. I think I'll keep my own powers and Lamont can keep them too, as a gift, you know, to pay you back for the food and stuff," M stammered and tried to get up from the table, but Layto was having none of that.

"Don't be silly Mr. M! You need this power boost, go ahead! Drink up," he walked closer to M, trying to force him to drink the blood.

"No, I really don't-no seriously, stop-STOP!" M yelled out again and a visible electric current erupted from his body. The current hit several objects in the room; brought the metal cart in the corner closer to the two, fried the monitors near both operating tables, and caused the lights to flicker. In particular, a heavy pan on the shelf behind Layto came flying towards the source of the electric current. Unfortunately for Layto, he was between the pan and M and it struck him in the head, knocking him out cold. M stared in shock for only a moment at this new display of power, but decided not to question it. He threw the vial with Lamont's blood in it against the wall and ran from Layto's home and out of the town.

He didn't know what would happen to either of the two when he left, or if they would come looking for him later, but one thing was for certain; if the Power Blood transfer was the only way for him to get strong enough to beat De and be leader again, he didn't want it anymore.

Still Divided

"Who are you? What are you doing in my house?!" A middle aged man rose from his armchair by the television and stared at his son and his new friend.

"You his dad?" Rod asked, gesturing to the kid who had led him into their home.

"Who wants to know?"

"I'll take that as a yes. My name is Rod, I don't want much from you; I just need to know what you know about the Pru Empire-"

At the name of his former employer, the man got visibly upset and started cursing quite loudly. "Get out, GET OUT!" he screamed. His son jumped and ran out of the room, but Rod held strong. He quickly scanned the living room, but there was no water in sight. If this turned to a fight, he would have to do it the natural way....

"No way dude. You have information I need. Look, I'm not trying to start anything, I just-Hey!" he had to stop talking very quickly, since the man rushed towards Rod trying to force him out of the house. Rod shoved the man off of him, and pushed him down when he tried to tackle him again.

The man huffed and puffed from the carpet near his couch, and used the corner of an end table to balance himself.

Rod prepared for the man to rush him again, but he just sat on the floor. "If you are here to recruit me to work for that thing then you can just kill me now. I left that life behind a long time ago."

Rod was a little taken aback by this. "What? No, I don't work for A.G. I want her gone just as much as anybody else. In fact, you might be able to help me beat her, depending on what you have to say," he bent down and helped the man to his feet to show that there were no hard feelings. The man thanked Rod and went back to his chair. Rod sat on the edge of the couch and waited for the man to start talking.

"What do you need to know?" he said finally.

"As much as you wanna tell. Mostly why is A.G. tryna bring the Empire back? Is she working for your old bosses? Who's behind this?" Rod said.

The man sighed. "I was a low level business man when the Pru Empire was a big deal. I was one of the people who did recruiting for new members of the Empire. We did a lot of the ground work in building up their domination. I'm sure your history books told you that the Empire got strong by supporting a bunch of different operations, right?" Rod nodded, so he continued. "Well that was the cover-up. We fed money to different businesses so that pretty much all the major corporations owed us. A lot. See, Ron and Carrie Prudence, the husband and wife that started the Empire, wanted to rule the world different from how anybody else did. They were trying to control everything business wise, and they were doing it until the Elementals-"

"All that is in my history book, too. I want to know who's getting A.G. to try and bring it back *now*," Rod cut him off.

The man looked at Rod, tapped his foot in agitation, and decided to jump ahead. "When the Elementals took down the Empire, they made only one mistake: they left the Ron and Carrie's kids alive. They used to live around here in fact, but they disappeared a while back and no one has seen them since. Everybody around here believes that they are the reason why A.G. is talking about the Pru Empire, so everybody that was working for them back in the day is either excited about getting back in the Empire or nervous that they are going to be killed for abandoning it," The man looked nervously at Rod. "Are you..."

Rod shook his head. "I already told you I don't work for A.G., so I really don't care that you 'betrayed' her bosses. But..." Rod patted his pocket, just vaguely enough for the man to think he still had the piece that the androids took from him back in the Rockdale Prison. The man's eyes widened and he looked from Rod's face to his pocket. He knew the others would never approve of this, but he was tired of walking everywhere.

"New plan: You got a car?" the man nodded again. "Good, because you and me are about to go for a little ride," Rod got up from the couch.

The man looked up at Rod. "You know you look real familiar."

"And?" Rod raised an eyebrow.

"And you have a bad temper. That's not good to have nowadays. Not with that thing running around and the Elementals back too,"

Rod grinned. "Yeah yeah, come on dude. We've got a long ride to take," Rod said, walking towards the door. The others would have to go to Grandia eventually, and he would meet them there.

***

Don ducked behind a building that looked like a place of worship. He had to squeeze between the very back of the building and a fence, but hopefully this place would be sacred enough to keep the angry mob from following him there too. He listened intently, too scared to look around the building and see were they still behind him. He heard the sound of someone walking through the dirt along the side of the building and held his breath in hopes that they didn't see him there, or at least that he would have enough time to get away from whoever it was.

"He's not here! Let's go!" a voice that sounded like the mob's leader called. Whoever was on the side of the building turned around and left before he could find Don wedged behind it.

Don waited a few more minutes and began trying to squeeze out from between the fence and the building. Without adrenaline pushing him, the process became a lot more difficult. "I'm going on a diet when this is over..." Don muttered to himself. He finally got out of his predicament and walked carefully along the side of the building. He looked left and right, but saw no one in either direction. He patted the bricks of the building and whispered "Thank you."

Curiosity got the better of him and he walked inside of the building and sat on a bench at the very back. There were a few people scattered on benches in front of him, but none of them looked up when he walked in: the patrons were too busy praying in what Don recognized as the native language of the Underground Kingdom. He reached into his bag to find his navigation tool; he knew he was in Rockdale still, but in his hurry to outrun the mob he had forgotten to check street signs.

"Lost?" a woman's voice asked him.

Don jumped, but laughed at himself. He looked up and into the vibrant brown eyes of the woman who had spoken. Her complexion was a shade darker than Don's but her accent screamed Underground Kingdom.

"My name's Sandra, I'm one of the facilitators here. You don't look like you're from around here," she said, taking in his attire. Compared to the more modest looking clothing that many of the people in the building wore, the brightly colored Skin Armor he designed for himself certainly stood out. "Do you need something, Mr....?"

Don nodded. "Don. Actually, I am a little lost-" he began.

Sandra barreled on. It seemed "lost" was a trigger word for her. "It seems as if you are lost in more than one way...we get a lot of kids your age in nowadays. Their parents have either been shipped off to work in the factory, or killed for not doing it. We can give you a place to stay for a little while, if you need it." Don looked around the building. He saw someone in one of the front rows that looked like the Alcon store owner he and the Elementals saw the last time they were there.

He looked back at Sandra. "Thank you, thank you very much, but I really need to get back home. You see, I'm from Rumas, and I have to..." the events of the day replayed in Don's mind. His eyes watered a bit as he thought about Del laying in front of the factory and the fact that he had did that to another person. He tried to wipe his eyes before Sandra saw.

She said nothing, but stooped down to hug him. Don returned the gesture as best he could. "Are you sure you don't want to stay here for a little while? These are rough times; you really shouldn't be out on your own…"

Don shook his head. "No, I need to get back home. Could you tell me how to get to Rumas from here?" He had found his navigation tool, but the long time between recharges left it powerless.

"The entrance to the above ground path should be two streets down and to your left about three blocks," Sandra said "But please remember, Don, if you ever feel lost, feel free to come back here. I'll be glad to help you however I can."

"I definitely will, Sandra. Thank you," Don packed his bag back up and left the building.

"Don! What are you doing back? Are you ok? Don's parents were more than a little surprised to see their son at the door when he finally got back home about a few hours later.

"I'm just, um, making a pit stop," Don explained. "Do you think you can drive me to Grandia?" Don asked his mother.

"Well, yes I can, but not tonight. Since you're here you should get a good night's rest." Mrs. Henton said.

Mr. Henton looked suspiciously at his son; he wasn't used to him being so quiet and somber. "Are you sure you're okay, son?"

Don had to fight hard to put a smile on his face. The words of the mob back in Rockdale kept running through his mind: the words "killer" and "liar" kept popping up. "I'm fine, Dad. I'm just gonna go to my room and go to sleep now. Wake me up when you're ready to drop me off in the morning." He went to sleep with the thought that once this was over he would have to pay Sandra another visit…

***

"So let me get this straight," De began again. He sat in

the middle of a huge antechamber surrounded by monks who sighed collectively at his words. They all looked at Nustaf, who had to have explained this to De at least three times. "The Orange Scepter was held here..." he pointed at the temple around him.

"Right," Nustaf said.

"...in the Shrine of Kashiro..."

"Yes,"

"...and it was stolen by these Prudence people and A.G...."

"Correct,"

"...in order to give A.G. the power to rule the whole continent, or the world if she wanted too."

"Yes, my friend. With the Orange Scepter's power she has been able to bring Redd Continent almost completely under her control. The only thing that stops her from being able to take over the rest of the world is that the other continents also have Mystic Items that they could use to defeat her," Nustaf explained.

"Ok, I get that. You also said that the Orange Scepter has a flaw, now explain that one to me again," De asked.

It was another monk that decided to answer this question. Even through his high pitched voice De noticed an accent that reminded him of Del's. "Yes sir. The Orange Scepter, along with the other Mystic Items, was made to aid the Elementals to defeat evil. By that design, legend tells us that they are unable to kill those with Elemental blood. This is why-"

"-this is why you guys think that we *have* to get the Orange Scepter back from A.G., because only we can," De finished, and the monk nodded. "Are you guys sure this is true?

I mean, I don't want us to run into the fight thinking we're invincible and one of us gets blown up…"

The monk looked nervous. "Well, it *is* legend that tells us this, so we can't be entirely certain. We have no reason to believe that our ancestors would lie to us."

"Yeah, that's comforting…" De said sarcastically. The idea would be nice; they could snatch the Orange Scepter from A.G., beat her, and get Prof. Peters out of jail. "Ok, so even if that works, what about my friend's dad? He created A.G. Not for all of this, but the police won't believe that. They're probably gonna keep him locked up for all of this," De remembered Rod explaining how the police would try to handle the situation after A.G. was finally brought down.

"Any one of us could testify that this was purely an attempt by the Pru Empire to claim the Orange Scepter again. We don't think any Elemental or any member of their family had anything to do with this," Nustaf said.

"Okay that sounds…wait, again?" De interjected.

"Yes, when the Pru Empire was originally in power they sent their agents from the Pewter Guard to try to take the Scepter by force. If it had not been for the past Elementals they would have succeeded. We are eternally grateful to all Elementals for that," he explained.

Even De knew about the Pewter Guard. They were originally a branch of the Pru Empire marketed as a team of highly trained operatives who were employed to the richest and most powerful people in the world as body guards, security personnel, and bouncers. Behind the scenes however, they also trained assassins and hit men. They were supposedly disbanded by the Racksons' generation of Elementals once the Pru Empire fell.

"So one of you will go to Rumas and tell the police what really happened?" De asked.

"Yes, in fact, I will go," Nustaf declared. "I'll get in the car and head there now."

De did a double take. "Wait, car? I thought monks were like, primitive and stuff?"

The group of monks all laughed. "No, Mr. Elemental. At least, not us. We may be monks but we do live in Redd Continent. We have access to some types of technology," one of them answered.

"We must have a way to restock food and other necessities for ourselves, so my brother got some of his friends to donate something," the monk speaking now did so with such perfect enunciation that it was clear he had a very privileged life before he became a monk. De couldn't help but picture M as a monk while he spoke.

"Speaking of Grandia," Nustaf began. "Didn't you say that you had to get there? To destroy the last factory?" De nodded. "You should take the car then, I shall find another route. You can drive, can't you?"

De had never driven a day in his life, but had the basic idea from riding with his parents, foster parents, and the other Elementals. Nevertheless the idea of doing it made him excited. "Yes, of course!" he said. How hard could it be?

It turned out to be a lot harder than he thought, especially at night. He managed to get away from the Shrine without any major incident, but driving straight across the sandy roads of Phorbes and the busy streets of the Great Lands proved to be pretty hard. De kept accidently swerving and almost hitting everything from buildings to people.

"Sorry! Sorry!" De said every time. Even though he felt bad, he had to admit that flying cross country at high speeds in a black drop-top was a level of fun that he had never imagined. The car got excellent mileage, so much that he only had to stop twice to fill it up even though he was driving nearly across the continent.

He was racing towards the borders of Grandia so quickly that he almost didn't notice M walking on the side of the road. He screeched to a halt a few feet in front of him and backed up (he had gotten plenty of practice backing away from obstacles earlier).

"Hey little guy! Where you been?" he asked M, but the latter said nothing. "Hey! It's me! Where are you coming from this early in the morning?" De tried to catch his attention but M just kept walking.

"HEY!" De yelled. He drove forward to catch up to M. Unfortunately, he swerved a little bit and got uncomfortably close to the young Elemental.

"Watch it you idiot!" M screamed.

"Well, at least I know you're not mute," De said. M just looked at him. "Come on dude, it was a joke, get in. You're heading to Grandia too right? You don't have to walk the whole way."

M contemplated this for a moment. "I guess it is safer for me to be inside the death mobile than outside," He reached out for the door handle and got in.

"Alright! Well to Grandia we go!" De said happily, bringing the car back to life and speeding onwards to their destination, with M panicking by his side.

Revelations

Mo's look of triumph only lasted a moment. He was definitely much stronger in the cold northern country of Grandia, but even here he couldn't control the freezing air enough to stop androids for long. As the android he was currently facing started to break out of its slowed state, Mo turned tail and ran...smack into another android. He reached towards this new threat, and thankfully was able to slow this android's movements as well. He easily ran around this android to get out of range of either of their laser blasts by the time they started firing them. He kept running and running until he was back in Greater Grandia's downtown area.

"I've got to stop doing this," Mo told himself. Ever since he realized where he was late yesterday he had been trying to get close to the factory, but to no avail. He was able to convince a hotel manager to give him a room the night before and returned to the factory earlier that day. He already knew that would be where the most androids were, but what he didn't realize was that he wasn't strong enough to beat the androids when they attacked him. All he could do is slow them down and try to run past them, but each time he got scared and ran before he thought they would kill him. He kicked a can down the street as he walked, allowing his blonde hair to drape over his face as he sulked down the street.

It had been bad news after bad news ever since he got there. If he had known being an Elemental would mean so much work and depression, he would've looked for a way to give up his powers. Then it hit Mo again. He was an Elemental, whether he liked it or not, and he had a job to do. He was going to get in that factory and take it down by himself if he had to. He had relied on the others too much; and now everyone was depending on him. His dad, Lauryn, the entire world. He had powers too, and he would use them to do what he had to do.

With a renewed resolve, Mo turned back around and marched back to where he saw all the androids patrolling. When they saw him, the one closest to him approached him.

"Elemental Resistance! You will fall this time!"

Mo however, summoned all the strength he could and raised his hands to the android, intending to freeze him where he stood. The cooler air would surely help him. He concentrated and concentrated, but the oncoming android barely even slowed. Mo opened his eyes, realized this and tried to dodge him, but he got nicked by a laser blast and fell on the ground, nursing his exposed arm. The android lifted Mo by his neck and held him in front of his face.

"Prepare to be turned over to Queen A.G. Elemental Resistance," it threatened. Mo looked into the eyes of the android and struggled weakly, but he knew in the back of his mind that it was over.

"I'm sorry guys," he closed his eyes and whispered to no

one in particular. In the next second, he opened his eyes and found himself falling back to the ground. He looked up and realized that even though the android's hand was still around his collar, the actual android was staring in shock at the metal stump where his hand used to be. He looked where the android was looking and saw none other than Don, crouching not far from them with a scope on his eye and the stolen laser hand in his own.

***

"Don!!" Mo yelled in relief as the now one-handed android and the others with him raced away from the Don's firing.

"Hi Mo!" Don replied, and the two best friends ran to and hugged each other tightly. "Okay, we better get outta here before they come back with reinforcements, come on!"

Of course Mo didn't argue, so the two boys ran back out of the industrial district of Greater Grandia to the main parts of the city. Mo stared at Don as they walked; overjoyed to see his friend again. He was ecstatic that after everything that had happened, at least one of his loved ones was still the same person and still there for him. Don was now wearing his winter coat, with his backpack knocking against it as they ran. It was the presence of this familiar outerwear that made Mo realize why he was so happy to see him in the first place.

"Don where have you been? How did you get here?" he asked.

"Well…" the two boys stopped to stare at some maniac driver racing past them, and Don shouted a few choice words at him before he continued talking. "Well, after Del teleported you guys away-"

Don stopped talking again when the insane driver began

flying down the street in reverse. Luckily these roads were all but abandoned so when the sleek black car screeched to a halt beside them no one was hurt. Don opened his mouth to yell at the driver some more when he saw the tell-tale red hair.

"De!" both boys yelled as the Elemental leader beamed back at them.

"Hi guys!" De said. He hopped out over the door out of the convertible. He was clearly hyper from his joy riding. "What're you doing here?"

"Us? What about you? Where did you get the car? And aren't you *cold*?" Don questioned. He smacked De's still exposed arms.

"Me? Nah, I'm always hot," De explained. "Aren't *you* cold?" he looked at Mo, who was also only wearing his Skin Armor.

"I'm always cold," he answered.

"Fair enough," De smiled. "Oh, the car! I got it from the monks. They were glad to help. Who knew monks had rides this sweet?" De said, patting the car gently.

Don was still confused. "Monks...what?"

"Hop in, I'll explain back at this house I was in," De offered, but neither of the other two moved. "What's wrong?"

"Do you have a license, De?" Don asked

"I got a hero license, which means I have to do what it takes to save the world!" De said.

"Uh huh. Well that's not a *driver's* license, which I do have, which means I'm driving," Mo said. He motioned for De to go to the passenger's side.

"Hey, don't you want me to keep practicing driving?" De complained.

"No," Mo and Don said together. De's face fell.

"I tell you what, you can drive all you want *after* we take out the factory here," Mo offered. De brightened up almost instantly and willingly went to the passenger side.

"Great...now if A.G. doesn't kill us De will," Don muttered as he sat in the backseat.

Once they arrived at their destination De began explaining the situation. "I found this house a little while ago with nobody inside; I think nobody's been in it for weeks judging by the dust and spoiled food. Probably got out when the androids took over."

"So you're stealing houses now? I see Rod's rubbing off on you," Mo shook his head as they walked inside.

De grinned. "Can't blame Rod for this one Mo, I knew how to pick locks long before I met him."

"I ain't the source of all the evil in the world, you know," said Rod himself, emerging from the back of the house to greet his comrades.

"Rod! When'd you get here?" De was just as shocked as Mo and Don, but he hugged him anyway. Rod pushed him off of him.

"Right after you almost ran me over in that death trap you're driving. The streets are for cars dude, not the sidewalks."

"Sorry man, still getting used to driving," De apologized.

Rod shook his head. "Anyway, after I left my hotel room I saw you leaving this house, but you flew off and almost killed me before I could talk to you. I figured you would come back, so I got M to let me in and waited."

"M's here too? That's great! Now we're all together again!" Don grinned. It seemed the night at home had done him well; he was back to his overly excited self.

De grabbed his arm to calm him down. "Yep. And now that we're all here, we need to talk about our next move. Where is M?" he asked Rod.

"In the back sleeping. I'll go get him, I have some stuff to tell you guys anyway," he said.

"Me too," De, Don and Mo all said.

"Well, looks like it's recap time. This is just like one of those 'Previously On...' screens all the shows do..." Don said.

The five heroes had sat in various spots in the living room of the house to listen to each other's stories. Rod propped himself against the front door, Don and Mo sat on the couch, De sat in a large armchair in the corner, and M squatted on the floor in front of the television. After everyone finished, M sent a charge to it (the electricity was off in the entire house) and started watching the news. They all watched for a moment to hear what was going on around them.

"...security tightens here in Greater Grandia as the city prepares for a visit from Resistance forces. No one is allowed within 150 feet of the factory until further notice. In unrelated news, a mysterious black convertible has been seen racing down the city streets..."

"Can you mute that or something?" De said loudly over Rod's laughing. M looked for a remote control, found it, and turned towards the others once the TV went silent.

"Ok, we still have to figure out what we're doing next. We now know who we need to look for after we beat A.G.," De began.

"The Prudence kids," Mo agreed.

"Yeah. But the question is, how do we find them? I

don't guess the old Pru Empire worker had any clue where they were now?"

Rod shook his head, making the few beads left on his braids click together. "Nope. Vilance said no one had seen them since before A.G. took over."

"That makes that a bust. At least for now," De shrugged.

"It's ok. We need to focus on beating A.G. first. That will make it easier to clear my Dad's name," Mo said.

"Well, look at you. I remember when you were saying A.G. couldn't be beat, now you're saying it's the first thing on the to-do list," De teased. Mo grinned slightly, as did Don beside him.

"Well, since you said the Orange Scepter probably won't blow us to smithereens, it seems a lot more possible," Mo explained. "And besides, with Prince Del gone-" Don's smile faltered a bit. "-she has one less henchman too."

"I guess this means you're ready to actually do something now?" Rod said.

"Shut up," Mo said coldly. Don also frowned at the Water Elemental, but Rod just shrugged.

"That reminds me, in all this talking we didn't hear from you two," Rod pointed at M and Mo. "So M, where did Del take you?" he asked.

M had been silent throughout the recap. "I don't want to talk about it," he said. He would rather not relive his escape from Layto and his night sleeping on the streets, especially since it wouldn't serve any purpose to the others.

"Oh come on, Sparky. Everyone else is having story time, why don't you join in?" Rod pressed, but M just shook his head.

"Let's just say that I won't be trying any more 'get

strong quick' schemes," he said bitterly. He glanced at De for a second and then turned back to the television. When it was clear he wasn't talking anymore De changed the subject.

"Well, what have you been up to Mo? Did you spend the entire time here in Greater Grandia?"

Mo nodded. "I did, and I found out something insane..."

"Lauryn's on TV!" M yelled suddenly, pointing at the screen. "Look!"

"Unmute it!" De said, and they soon heard Lauryn talking to the reporter.

"...I assure the people of Grandia that even though the rebellion forces bear down on our city, the hand of Queen A.G. is strong, and will not bend to these Elementals." Lauryn turned her face to the public. "The people of Grandia will be safe, and the rule of Queen A.G. will continue to bring the prosperity of the Pru Empire to our land." The interview ended, and the reporter began discussing the weather. M muted the television again and they all turned to Mo to see his reaction. Surprisingly, he was not emotional or shocked in any way at his mother figure's apparent betrayal.

"I guess that pretty much sums up what I found out," he said sadly. "Lauryn's acting as president of Grandia. And she's being controlled by A.G."

Retaking Grandia

De shoved the doors to the President's office open and all five boys walked inside. The lavish sky blue office was empty however, and they realized that all the androids they went through to get in here were a waste.

"I thought you said she would be here?" Rod asked Mo.

"I thought she would be here," he replied. He approached the large chair behind the desk at the back of the room. It looked as if it hadn't been used or moved in days.

"Well she's not here. Spread out guys, maybe we can find any clues as to where she went," De ordered. They all began searching the room, but their efforts were unsuccessful.

"I'm not finding anything," M said from behind a fish tank.

"Me either," Rod called, putting books back on their shelves.

"I don't think there's anything here," Don said. He had sat down in the President's plush chair to search the desk.

"Well there has to be something!" Mo cried. He had not stopped searching.

Don and M looked at De, and he nodded. Rod shrugged but agreed as well. "Mo...I know you want to find Lauryn, but we can't stay here looking for clues that aren't here, especially when we have a job to do."

Mo stopped rummaging through city documents. As much as he hated to admit it, De was right. "Ok. We do have to destroy the factory. It's the reason why we all came here in the first place. We have to take down this last factory so that A.G. can't make any more androids."

De looked relieved that he understood. "Yes exactly."

"Then, once we find A.G. we can make her tell us what she did to Lauryn and where she put her," Mo finished. Rod raised an eyebrow but De agreed and nodded. "So, let's go to the factory."

"You know where it is?" M asked.

"Of course. I came here with my Dad back when they were first building it, both of us did," Mo gestured towards Don.

"Wait, this factory was here before A.G. took over? Why?" De asked.

Don decided to answer. "President Hammock had all intentions of mass producing the android guards after he tested his own. He was hoping to finally have some way to put the Pewter Guard out of business. As part of the deal, he was having the factory built with Prof. Peters' consent so that they could start as soon as possible. I guess it just made a lot of sense for A.G.'s forces to use this factory to produce some of those first androids."

"Well, if you guys know where it is, lead the way," De

said.

"Why on Colorius did you bring a drop top to Grandia?! Don't you know it's freezing here?" M complained. Even with the top up, it was quite cold in De's new ride. He shrugged from the passenger seat.

The three in the back seat were bundled together for warmth, as even with coats on (the previous owners of their house had left clothes; luckily M and Rod were able to fit in them), the nighttime air was much colder than any of them expected. Unfortunately for them, none of them had Mo or De's resilience to temperature change and the vehicle's heater wasn't working. De offered to sit in the backseat with them, in hopes that his natural heat would warm them up, but M all but fought him for suggesting it. Right about now he was having second thoughts about his stubbornness.

"At least it's a nice ride, through the city I mean," Don's teeth chattered as he spoke. He peered around at the capital city. Even at night it was lit up with the lights inside houses, and the moonlight shone beautifully on the city's infamous sky blue architecture. Greater Grandia, as a whole, was everything to be expected from the capital city of the richest country on Redd Continent. The streets were paved perfectly with smooth stones, and each house looked like a brightly colored ice sculpture in the light given off by the many lampposts on each corner; they provided a golden glow that cast the shadow of the city's trademark double G below them.

"How far are we?" Rod asked through his scarf.

"Almost there. We're gonna park in this alley way and walk the rest of the way," Mo answered.

"Walk?!" M shrieked. "It's like 20 below out there, we'll

freeze!"

"Better we freeze than you get warmed up by some nice lasers," De said. "In this car we'd be sitting ducks too close to the factory. Besides, it's not *that* cold."

M grumbled and complained, but said nothing else out loud. Mo parked the car in the next alley and the five of them got out and started walking towards the last factory they had to destroy. Even down the road from the factory it was obvious that it would take a lot more than a few flames, bolts of electricity and well placed ice to bring such a huge and sturdy looking building down. It was guarded by a large iron gate with the double G's, inside of which sat a delicate looking fountain directly in front of the factory doors. One of the G's in the gate had been knocked out, and someone had tried to graft a crudely shaped 'A' in its place. It clashed with the entire design, but not as much as the androids inside of the gate did.

"Stop, Elemental Resistance! Surrender now and we will give you the privilege of allowing Queen A.G. to eradicate you herself!" one of the giant androids yelled from behind the fence. At least seven androids lined up in front of the factory's double doors as its first line of defense.

"How bout...no?" De taunted. He kicked open the gate and the others ran into it after him. M started flinging electricity at the androids to make them stagger, and though they retaliated with their laser attacks Don matched them as best he could with his own laser hand.

"Please have water inside, please have water inside..." Rod pleaded, focusing his attention on the fountain. He felt some not-yet-frozen liquid settled in the lower portion and silently thanked the Mystics for it. He sent some of the water rushing over the androids, and Mo followed up by freezing the water on the androids, effectively casing their limbs in ice.

"Guys, you should be able to stop them now!" Mo yelled happily, and sure enough, the propulsion from M, De and Don's attacks combined with the flash frozen metal made it much easier to blow the machines apart. The Elementals were easily able to take out the seven androids and get close to the entrance, when they heard loud footsteps coming from inside.

"Please don't tell me..." De said, but sure enough, the door was blown open by a gigantic laser blast and there stood another of the terrifying Battle Robots in its place.

"Don?" Rod looked to him, but Don shook his head.

"I can't shut it off without getting inside. If you guys can distract him..."

The thing powered up its jets, and started racing around the outside area of the factory. Rather than try to attack, the Elementals simply tried to avoid being trampled by the thing, but it seemed determined to get to one of them: Don. The machine easily caught up with the chubby hero, and smacked him away with its laser hand. The force of the blow, combined with the momentum from the thing flying around sent Don careening into the fence.

"DON!" Mo screamed. Unlike the Elementals, Don was not blessed with higher stamina and endurance so Mo abandoned all pretenses of the battle and ran to the fence, with the robot right behind him. Rod summoned more water to soak the thing, and M followed up with his strongest electric attack yet. The combination of the two's powers didn't defeat or even stop the thing, but it did take its attention off Don and Mo and placed it back on the other three Elementals. It raced towards them, jets blazing. M and De tried to hit it with their powers, but the thing just kept coming and De was far too panicked to focus on its flames again. The three started running around their battlefield with the machine in hot pursuit. The three stopped running right in front of the factory doors, and the robot stopped its jets; instead deciding to finish them off with a laser blast. With no way to protect themselves, the three Elementals had resigned themselves to their ends, when they heard Mo gasp from behind the robot.

"Rose!" he yelled, and sure enough, Rose Rackson had come running from the city towards the Battle Robot.

As Rose neared the robot, it turned to face its new opponent. It tried to fire a laser at Rose, but she was too quick for it. She dodged the attack and the swiping of its blade, and instead connected a powerful kick with its side. The kick was enough to knock the thing off balance, and Rod, seeing his chance, summoned the last of the water from the fountain to topple it over. Mo added to the attack by freezing that same water around the robot, giving M and De the chance to pelt it with their strongest attacks. For good measure, Rose ran and jumped on the chest of the large robot, and summoned all the strength she could to deliver a punch directly to what had to have been its core. Her fist broke through the flash frozen metal and directly into the robot, effectively putting an end to it.

Rose jumped off of the robot and dusted her hands off. "Well, that was thrilling," she said. De, M and Rod rushed to her side.

"Wow Rose! That was amazing!" De exclaimed. "I mean, I knew you were strong, but that was crazy!"

Rose looked at Rod. "You mean to tell me you watched me destroy all those androids back in Rumas and didn't tell your friends about it? Now what did we agree on? I saved you twice in there, and you have to tell everyone how wrong you were about me needing extra help. Don't think just because I've been gone a little while I forgot," Rose wagged her finger at Rod, who for once looked embarrassed.

"That actually brings up a good question Rose, how did you get here? We thought for sure you and Master Rackson were being guarded by A.G. herself. How'd you escape?" M asked.

"I'll explain once we get in the fac-Oh Mo, Don!" Rose's eyes had finally fallen on the two near the gate. Mo had finally gotten Don conscious again but he kept slipping in and out of it. His mouth bled and his leg bent at an unnatural angle, leaving Mo to have to help him move. It was a mark of his affection for his best friend that Mo found the strength to move him at all.

"You have to go to the hospital!" Rose insisted. "I'll take him, Mo. You go inside with the others," she offered. She picked Don off of Mo's shoulders and put him on hers, which brought Don a little closer to the ground than before.

"Are you sure? I could go...the city is probably dangerous..." Mo said. Rose looked at Rod and cleared her throat. He sighed.

"Rose Rackson is a highly capable Cosmic Elemental. Having faced the evil Kwan and brought down the Pru Empire alongside the rest of Generation Immortal., she is fully able to handle any challenge when armed with her physical prowess and ability to draw on the energy of the cosmos," Rod muttered.

"Couldn't have said it better myself," Rose grinned at him. "Anyway, trust me; the four of you will want to go inside to see what's in there. I'll be back soon," she turned to carry

Don to the hospital.

"Should we follow her anyway, just in case?" M asked.

"We *do* need to go on take out this factory," De
answered.

"Besides, the longer I'm away from her the less I have to
boost her ego. I'm supposed to do this for two weeks!" Rod
complained.

M laughed and playfully shoved Rod. "Dang you must've
really needed saving in that first factory!"

"Let's just go in already," Rod walked ahead of them
and thrust the doors to the factory open.

Much like the factory in Rockdale, the first floor of the
Greater Grandia factory was mostly empty. As the Elementals
looked around, however, they did notice two people in the
room. One was strapped to the assembly line, and the other
was nearer to them, sitting with his head in his hands on the
stairs.

"Lauryn!" Mo screamed, recognizing the figure on the
table as his android mother figure. The other person looked up
at the Elementals.

"I thought you people would never get here," the Silver
Man half grinned and stood up.

"What have you done to her?" Mo demanded. He
walked ahead of the other three and closer to the Silver Man.

He looked over at her and shrugged. "I had to restrain
her; she was causing too much trouble."

"I bet she fought you off! I bet that was the only way
you could get her down, I'll kill you!" Mo rushed towards the
Silver Man, with the others right behind him. The Silver Man
stretched his arms out to hold Mo at bay.

"Wait, listen to me!" he yelled, but the Elementals were not taking any chances. M shot the Silver Man's arms with electricity and De did the same with his fire, forcing the Silver Man to let Mo go. When the Silver Man looked around and noticed that Rod was approaching Lauryn he threw an arm out to stop him, which De and M promptly shot at again. Rod got the message, however, and rejoined the group.

"Why should we listen to you?" De asked finally. "You've done nothing but try to kill us since we met you, what's changed now?"

"A lot," the Silver Man said.

"Yeah right! You're still a bad guy, and you've hurt Lauryn!" Mo yelled. "Why won't you let her go?"

The Silver Man sighed. "Fine. Go get her."

The four Elementals looked at each other and the Silver Man for a moment, but when he sat back on the stairs M and De slowly walked over to go untie the android. Mo stood his ground, staring daggers at the Silver Man once again with his head in his hands. Rod stood by as well, watching the Silver Man's movements. All of a sudden, Mo leapt towards the Silver Man, only to be stopped by Rod.

"Let me go! What, are you two working together? LET ME GO!" he snapped at him.

"Dude I'm saving your life, you rush him and he's gonna chop you up," Rod said plainly.

"Yeah right, you two probably have some agreement or something, get off!" he stamped Rod's foot, and when Rod yelled out and let him go he ran towards the Silver Man and started punching him. Instead of slicing him up like Rod thought he was going to do, the Silver Man actually just took the blows Mo threw at him. M and De abandoned trying to carry Lauryn over and rushed to help Mo while Rod began to look for the coolant tank in this factory to help as well.

"Stop!" Master Rackson said from the second floor of the factory. At his voice all five boys stopped fighting and looked up at him. They were all frozen in shock at his sudden appearance: Rod was in the middle of pulling Mo off of the Silver Man, who had fallen on the stairs while defending himself against Mo's punches. M and De had stopped a couple feet from the Silver Man, waiting for Rod to pull them apart so they could keep hitting him with their own attacks. "Morgan, I would very much like for you would stop hitting my son."

Rod dropped Mo and the four Elementals looked at each other: after all, they had all been told a certain story about Master Rackson's eldest son's current whereabouts.

"You told us your son was dead. We thought he got killed by A.G.," Mo said after a while.

"Yeah well he lied. Get used to it; he does that a lot," the Silver Man muttered, not looking at any of them.

"You don't even look like Lucas," M said.

"You seem to forget my son is a Morph Elemental, Maurice. He can alter his appearance at will. I also technically did not lie. When Lucas ran away from home, the last thing I told him was that he was dead to me. I never said he was killed by A.G." Master Rackson said quietly. He had joined his son at the foot of the stairs and tried to help him up, but Lucas snatched away from him.

"I'm fine. And I guess now since everyone knows there's no need for this anymore." He got up and closed his eyes. Almost immediately the black dreadlocks shrunk into his skull and turned into short and messy brown hair. His muscles started to shrink and he shot upwards in height to at least six feet. The silver colored skin turned from its inhuman color to a more tanned tone a little darker than Master Rackson's, and the eyes that had closed as the dark brown ones of the Silver Man reopened as Lucas Rackson's hazels.

De watched this transformation and nudged M, who was standing nearest to him. "So...this guy is Master Rackson's other son?" M rolled his eyes and nodded. "Well, why is he working for A.G.?"

"I am right here you know. You could ask me," Lucas snarled. "I left home because he loves his students more than his son."

"Seriously? Daddy issues?" Rod said. He shook his head and walked away from the group, but Lucas followed him.

"You think that's all that's wrong? That I have 'daddy issues'? I bet that's easy for you to say, Rod. He absolutely adores you. He was always talking about the progress you've made, even now, when we were on our way here, all he could talk about was how much you four have done; it's that same simple mindedness that ran Mom off," Lucas' voice shook with barely suppressed anger; it was clear that these were things he had wanted to say for a long time. "I joined A.G. to show him that I am worth him talking about, that I am just as good, if not better than any one of you. I have been training for three years to have all the power I have, but you four get all the praise and you just showed up, you get all the attention and I get nothing. Do you know how what that is like?"

M walked away from the stairs as well, but kept his eyes on the group. He could understand, at least in some parts, Lucas' feelings of inferiority. De stood near to Mo, just in case he tried to jump Lucas again, but he too, could understand the Morph Elemental's desire for a parent's love.

Rod didn't seem to be in as understanding a mood. He hadn't turned back to look at Lucas as he spoke. "Dude, I barely even have a Dad, you should be glad that yours can choose to ignore you."

Mo wasn't moved either. "What does this have to do with Lauryn? Why did you have to hurt her to get attention from your dad?"

"This wasn't his plan, it was mine. She had to be deactivated for her own good, and yours. She was planning to lure you all here and destroy the factory with you inside of it." Master Rackson explained. The Elementals all looked on in shock.

"Where is Aunt Rose? She went into the city to warn you," Lucas asked suddenly.

"She took Don to the hospital, he was beat up pretty bad by the robot thing," M explained.

"Is Donald alright?" Master Rackson asked. Particularly he was asking Mo, but Mo couldn't take his eyes off Lucas and Lauryn.

"I think he'll be ok. He was bleeding pretty bad though," Rod answered.

Master Rackson approached Mo. "Morgan..." he started.

"If we boot her back up, will she be the same?" Mo asked. His eyes had not left Lauryn.

"Yes. I made sure of that," Master Rackson confirmed.

"Okay well this is all well and good, the Silver Man is a Rackson and we found Lauryn, but we still have to bring this place down, don't we? And what is he-" M pointed at Lucas "-gonna do for us? How do we know that he's not gonna double cross us?"

Lucas had grabbed Lauryn's body and walked back up to the others. "Well, like he said Lauryn was going to bury you here, so we think she must have put some kind of bomb in here somewhere. Did you find it?" he asked his father. When he nodded Lucas continued. "Is it still working?" Master Rackson nodded again and Lucas pulled a small device from Lauryn's hand. "Let's go outside then."

The two Racksons walked outside, with the other four Elementals following behind them. They kept walking until they were outside the gates. "Cover us," Lucas said to Master Rackson.

"Kareema Rhama Heximae!" Master Rackson yelled, holding his hands towards the gate. From his fingertips the flashing multicolored energy spread to the gate and surrounded them. Lucas then pressed the single button on the detonator, and the younger Elementals watched in awe as several explosions went off in the factory, reducing it to rubble in moments. Master Rackson dropped his shield as the dust settled, and Lucas turned to his fellow Elementals.

"Does that answer your questions?" He said to M.

"Ok, well that was pretty cool," M relented.

"Sounds like a 'welcome to the team' to me," De said, shaking Lucas' hand.

"Yeah, welcome to whatever this is," Rod said. Mo nodded in Lucas' direction and the five of them started to walk away when Master Rackson grabbed his son's shoulder. Lucas shrugged him off.

"What," Lucas asked. He turned to see the look on his father's face.

"Son...I'm proud of you. I know I don't say it enough, but I am. Good job," Master Rackson's eyes supported the truth of his words.

"Yeah, well, took long enough," Lucas answered. He had looked away from his father.

"I understand that I have made some mistakes-"

"Try a lot."

"Alright, *a lot* of mistakes. But don't think that I don't care for you. You are my son; I will always be proud of you and from now on I will try my best to show it," Master Rackson said. He patted Lucas on the back and turned to catch up to the others.

"I'll believe it when I see it," Lucas said to his father's back. He was used to his father's empty promises, but even now he couldn't help but feel a little better. He slowly followed his father to his aunt's car, which was parked in a separate alley from the Elemental's transportation, and they left the smoking remains of the final factory behind them.

Search

"Aww man! It was just like the reunion between Baltalla and her father on *Baltalla: Guardians of the Keystone*! I hate I missed it!" Don groaned. In only a short while the doctors had bandaged his wounds, reset his leg, and hooked him to a couple machines to monitor his recovery. When the Elementals came to see him he was well enough to sit up on his hospital bed and listen to the riveting tale, but the doctors were forcing him to stay another night so the other seven decided to stay in Greater Grandia with him until they could all leave.

"Some things don't change," M laughed.

"The doctors said he wasn't beat up *too* bad. They gave him some pain medicine and told him to try to rest for a few days and stay on the androids' good side," Rose explained. She sat happily on the couch in the room between her brother and nephew.

"Guess I'm just gonna have to disobey them, huh? Now that the factories are gone we can go take out A.G.!" Don said happily.

"No Donald," Master Rackson said. "You are already hurt, you need to do as your doctors have instructed and rest."

Don's face fell.

"Aw come on! Can't I at least watch?" he begged.

"I agree with him. A.G. would waste no time taking you out if you were with us, you have to stay out of the fight, for your own safety," Mo had been fairly quiet since they left the factory, but he spoke up to try to keep his friend out of harm's way. Don sighed and laid back on his bed.

"It's late," M said, looking out at the night sky. "It's gotta be after midnight by now."

"Yeah, we should go back to the house and get some rest," De got up from his stool and started walking to the door.

"Do you need any of us to stay here with you tonight, Don?" Rose asked.

"No, I'll be alright. You guys go get your rest. I'll see you in the morning."

"Hopefully we'll all be here tomorrow," Mo said. He was obviously referring to Lauryn, who De and Lucas had driven back to the safe house before meeting the others at the hospital. Now they all hopped in either De's convertible or Rose's car and headed back to their temporary home for some much needed sleep.

Mo hopped out of the car first and ran into the house. He retrieved the still deactivated Lauryn from the closet and brought her to the living room floor.

"Anxious, aren't you?" Rod asked, but Mo ignored him.

"How do I reactivate her?" he asked Lucas.

Lucas stepped forward and turned his index finger into an oddly shaped key. He unlocked a cavity under Lauryn's chest, and pulled her programming chip from his pocket. "When the Prudence kids reprogrammed her, they kept her old programming chip. I found it one day and have been holding on to it ever since," he handed the chip to Mo. "Put that in and give it a little while, once it loads back up she should be good as new."

"Well, you should place the chip in and come to bed, Morgan. We all need to rest. The search for A.G.'s whereabouts begins in a few hours," Master Rackson said.

"You guys go on, I'll be fine," Mo replied. Master Rackson nodded and he and the others all went to different parts of the house to get some rest. M curled up on the couch behind Mo.

"Try not to be too loud," he said kindly, but in a few minutes he was asleep.

Mo nodded, but still did not budge.

Hours passed, but Mo sat right where he was. A few times Lauryn's eyes flashed, but Mo wasn't sure if it was her trying to boot up or his imagination. The signs of sunrise were in the sky outside, and Mo was beginning to worry that her original programming chip must have been damaged. He might have lost her forever, after he had done so much to save her...

Mo got up to go to the bathroom and when he walked back into the living room, he couldn't help but scream at the sight: Lauryn was standing in the middle of the floor, looking confused as ever. M jumped up and fell off of the couch, and the others came running out of their rooms to see what was the matter. They all stopped and looked from Lauryn to Mo and back again.

"Morgan..." Lauryn said.

Mo was near tears of joy. He ran forward and the two hugged tightly. Rose Rackson sniffled in the background, while M muttered about having hurt his back falling off the couch.

"Morgan, where am I? Where are we? What's going

on?" Lauryn asked after a moment.

Mo wiped his eyes again. "That doesn't matter, all that matters is that you're here and you're you."

Lauryn looked at him suspiciously. "Of course I'm me, who else would I be?"

"You don't remember?" Mo asked.

"Remember what? The last thing I remember is storming the factory in Rumas and losing. Now I'm here. What happened?"

Mo started to answer, but Master Rackson coughed loudly. When the others looked at him, all he said was "Sorry, that's a downside you deal with at my age." Thankfully, Mo got the hint.

"Nothing. You're here in Greater Grandia because we saved you from A.G.'s forces. We just destroyed the last factory so now we're ready to take on A.G." Mo said. Technically he wasn't lying, but Lauryn still looked at him skeptically. She decided to let it go.

"You look...different Morgan. What have you been doing since I saw you last?"

Mo looked around at the others in the room. Truthfully, they all looked different in some way, and not just the ripped clothes and few scars from constant battle. He turned back and smiled at Lauryn. "You wouldn't believe me if I told you."

Even though Master Rackson wanted the search to start that day, he conceded that they could afford to take one more day to truly rest. This actually turned out to be a good thing, since Don had to spend another day in the hospital because the nurses found him trying to sneak out before he was discharged. The next morning Mo and Rose Rackson went to go pick up

Don, and when they came back they all gathered around the huge dining room table to discuss their next move. "We have to take Don and Lauryn back to Rumas, and maybe from there we can ask around to see where A.G. is, unless of course..." Master Rackson looked over at Lucas, who shook his head.

"The last time I saw A.G. we were here in Greater Grandia, plotting the protection of the last two factories, and if she were here she would have shown herself after the factory was destroyed," he answered.

"I'm not going to sit back and wait at home while you all go to face A.G.," Lauryn said.

Don saw his opportunity and jumped on it. "If Lauryn's going to the battle, I am too!"

"No way!" Mo said. "You're still on crutches and we can't let anything happen to either of you. You guys need to be safe, and safe for you two is away from the battle, and us."

The two wanted to keep arguing, but Master Rackson raised a hand for silence. "We must not allow A.G. the opportunity to create more casualties. I'm sorry, but Morgan is right, both of you must remain in Rumas."

"What about our safety?" M asked, "Are we sure we can take out A.G. now?"

"I agree with Sparky," Rod said. "I mean, yeah we kinda messed A.G. up by getting rid of the factories, but she's still strong as ever, plus she still has the Orange Scepter."

"Well, I told you what the monks said," De argued. "The Orange Scepter helps the Elementals, so we should have a chance against it."

"But no one knows if that is even really true," M countered.

"We might as well try," De said. "And since we don't

know where A.G. is, we could start looking in Rumas.

"Fine idea, Derren," Master Rackson agreed. "To Rumas, everyone."

"This is creepy…" M said. After dropping Don and Lauryn off at Don's house (and forcing them to stay), the Elementals began scouting the city for clues to A.G.'s current location. The streets of Rumas were unusually quiet, especially for it being early in the afternoon. They had seen a grand total of four cars on the roads, and no one, not protestors, not businessmen or children, was anywhere to be found in the alleys or the buildings. It seemed like in the many weeks the heroes had been gone everyone else in the city had left with them. Even when the factory was being built people still filled the streets and businesses in the huge city, but right now there was no sign of life: organic or mechanical.

"Rumas has never been this empty, something's wrong…" Rose said.

"There's the Café Rena, someone's bound to be in there!" Mo blurted out, pointing towards the fancy restaurant across the street from them.

"I highly doubt anyone who would know where A.G. is would be in there," Lucas said flatly.

"But right now it is our only option, there doesn't seem to be anyone else here," Master Rackson pointed out, so they went anyway.

The restaurant was empty as well, at least at first glance. The ornate red and gold chairs were still on top of the tables, and there was no maître d at the podium and no way to tell that anyone was inside.

"Wait…do you guys hear that?" M asked.

They all listened. "Yeah…I hear…somebody upstairs,"

Rod said, pointing up the stairs to another part of the restaurant.

"Perhaps if whoever it is cannot tell us about A.G. they can at least tell us why no one else is here," Master Rackson said, and the seven of them walked up the stairs and to the man whose back was turned to them. De walked a little closer and tapped him on the shoulder.

"Excuse me, sir?"

"Don't call me sir, we are the same age, you know," said Del, turning around to face the Elementals. He looked a lot less extravagant in only a t-shirt and some (still tight fitting) jeans.

"Del? What are you doing here? Why aren't you with A.G.?" Lucas asked.

"Is that you Silvy? I think I liked your other look better," Del said to Lucas.

Rod sighed. "Do any of you people stay dead?"

"Dead? Who said I was dead?" Del wondered.

"Well, Don kind of said it, but..." M said

"Oh, him. Yeah he did get me good with a laser. It was good some of my people decided to take me to a hospital. Got a couple cracked ribs and I can't teleport for a while, but I'm fine," Del leaned back to show the Elementals several large bandages on his torso.

"Ok, whatever, but why are you here?" De asked

"Oh, that one's simple. I'm here to help," Del dove back into his plate.

"Yeah right. Why would you want to help us now?" Rod asked.

"Actually, I tried to help you back in Rockdale, but you didn't want to listen, did you De?" Del turned towards the Elemental leader. De suddenly remembered Del wanting to talk to him when they teleported deeper into the underground city. "Besides, didn't you all enjoy the vacations I sent you on? Didn't you get valuable info from them?"

De, Mo, and Rod thought about where they were dropped off. They had all gotten information from their "vacations" that was useful to their mission. M, however, felt cheated.

"I didn't learn anything! You set me up!" he complained.

"You mean to tell me you didn't meet that madman Layto? You didn't learn about the Power Blood ritual and how he used it to give powers to Samantha Prudence? That's how they were able to get in and mess up A.G. in the first place. You were supposed to stop that quack," Del said in between mouthfuls of food. Everyone looked at M.

"Nope, not at all," he lied. "It was a dead end; I think you were off by a couple miles."

Del shrugged. "Oh well, three out of four ain't bad."

"Ok well clearly you've been playing both sides just like Lucas was, but why are you here now?" Rose asked.

"You people are looking for A.G. right? I know where she is," Del picked up his burger and bit a big chunk out of it.

"Well? Where is she?" Rod asked impatiently.

"In your house," Del said, pointing his fork at the three Racksons. All of their jaws dropped.

"She's at Rackson Manor? Why?" Mo asked.

"When she sent me to Rockdale she said that since you guys kept taking things from her, she was gonna take something from you. I thought it just meant she was gonna kill you guys, but taking over your house makes more sense. It's kinda poetic, really." Del said.

Everyone took a moment for Del's words to settle in. Everyone except Lucas, who asked "Were you planning on helping her again?" He alone knew what Del was willing to do to save himself from A.G.'s wrath.

"Nah, I'm done playing hero or villain. I'm going back to my cushy prince job. I just came here to find you guys to tell you about A.G. Then I got hungry so...yeah," Del laughed and kept eating.

"Is that why the city is so empty; I would assume everyone's in hiding?" Master Rackson asked, to which Del only nodded.

"She plans on turning your house into a factory since you destroyed all of hers. Well, she decided it when she still had factories, but you know what I mean. She's probably waiting there with her army of androids and Battle Robots for you to show up."

"Well that means we must go there, immediately," Master Rackson said.

"Yeah! We gotta get our house back!" Rose agreed.

They all ran down the stairs to leave the restaurant, leaving only Lucas and Del upstairs. "Are you coming?" Lucas asked him.

"Nah, I'll leave this to the real heroes," Del responded.

Lucas chuckled. "I'm no more of a hero than you are, I worked for her too. At least you did it to protect your country; I only did it to get back at my father."

"Yea, but you're an Elemental, you would've done the right thing eventually anyway," Del looked down at his plate. "Besides...I really don't wanna be on that thing's bad side again," he said seriously.

"I understand," Lucas said. "Thank you, Del."

SEARCH

"Don't mention it. Besides, I gotta go back home and help my Dad fix up the Kingdom," Del stopped eating and got up from the table.

"Good luck," Lucas said, sticking out his hand.

"Same to you Silvy," Del said, shaking it.

Del grabbed what was left of his plate and followed Lucas outside where they finally parted ways. Del kept walking into the city while Lucas joined the others on their walk to Rackson Manor, the place where their journey would finally end: with either their victory or A.G.'s.

225

Battle at Rackson Manor

Rackson Manor, huge and slightly creepy by normal standards, looked positively ominous sitting on its hill beyond the vast gate now. The house itself looked like it normally did, but with two huge Battle Robots patrolling the pathway and a number of androids standing around the manor it was surely not the same mansion they left all those weeks ago.

"I can't believe she's using our house as a base! How dare she!" Rose spat. The heroes had stopped at the road just before the gate to plot their attack.

"We can make her pay once we are inside," Master Rackson assured her.

"Do we have a plan to make her pay?" Mo asked.

"Of course we do," De said. "We go in, guns blazing, and take out the androids. A.G. will come out, and we'll let you and M distract her, while Rod uses his sticky fingers to swipe the Orange Scepter. Without that, she'll go down like any other android."

"That actually sounds like a good plan, really, but one small issue: why do I have to be the one stealing from the killer android?!" Rod yelled as loud as he could without attracting attention.

"Well, there's no water around, so you're gonna have to rely on your other talents," De looked somewhat apologetic.

"Besides, you have the best chance of actually stealing from her. You have the most experience," Mo pointed out.

Rod wasn't so easily convinced. "Yes, but not stealing in plain sight from someone who could kill me in the blink of an eye!"

"You'll be fine, we'll be covering you," M assured him.

"I should have just gone to jail, I'd be safer..." Rod groaned.

The seven heroes snuck to the gate and waited until the Battle Robots had turned their backs and gotten farther up the hill to start climbing it. They planned to get as close to the robots as they could before they started attacking them, since outside of A.G. they would be the most difficult opponents. Mo slipped going up the hill and fell face forward in the dirt.

"I *always* fall coming up here!" Mo whispered. De grinned and turned around to help his comrade up.

"WATCH OUT!" Lucas screamed. He stretched his arms to snatch the two out of the way of a huge laser blast. When the dust cleared around the crater where De and Mo had just been, they all looked towards the Manor to see that it was not one of the Battle Robots who fired the blast, but A.G. herself, standing on the second floor balcony. The android's trademark black ensemble accentuated her skin and blonde hair even more perfectly in the bright sun of the day, but her green eyes reminded the others just how dangerous this seemingly beautiful non-human was.

"You are intruding in my domain. Explain." A.G. said.

"*Your* domain? This is MY house, lady!" Rose roared.

"This 'house' is being used as a base of operations for the Pru Empire. It has been compromised. Soon, its former tenants will be no more," A.G. pointed the Orange Scepter at the heroes again; this time firing an insanely powerful laser blast at Rose. Lucas snatched his aunt away from danger just as he had done for De and Mo. This brought A.G.'s attention to her former employee.

"You have abandoned the glory of the Pru Empire to align yourself with the Elemental scum. Explain."

"I've 'always aligned myself' with them; to bring you down!" he yelled. Master Rackson couldn't help but smile at his son as he spoke.

"Let's get this over with, A.G.! Come down and fight us like a man! Er, woman, android...thing..." De added. The power of his words was brought down by his mistake, but it made the android no matter. Her voice stayed its chilling monotone despite the threats made to her.

"You are not worthy to witness the full glory of the Pru Empire. Your fates will be decided by its lower ranking agents. Goodbye, Elementals," she turned and walked back into the manor, leaving the heroes to contend with the Battle Robots and the androids, all of which had begun to approach the heroes, lasers at the ready.

"Kareema Rhama Heximae!" Master Rackson roared. His magical shield surrounded the heroes, protecting them from the many attacks of their enemies. Even he, however, struggled under the might of so many laser blasts.

"There's no way we can beat all of them and still put up a fight against A.G.!" Mo said.

"You're right, that's why you four will have to go inside

and go after A.G., leave these guys to us!" Rose pointed at herself and her family. Lucas nodded, but Master Rackson's attention was fully on trying to keep his shield up as the metal guardians drew ever closer.

"No way! We can't leave you guys out here!" M argued.

"We're gonna need all of us to take her out!" Rod said.

Rose smiled at him. "I think you've been singing my praises a little too much. You guys got this; you have a plan and everything you need on your side. This is what you've trained for."

"But," De began. One of the giant robots pounded on the bubble that was Master Rackson's shield, bringing the old master to his knees.

"No time to argue! You four are going and that's that!" Lucas snapped. The younger Elementals nodded.

"Now Matthew!" Rose yelled. Master Rackson cried out, sending the same energy from his shield across the area where all the androids and robots stood. The wave of magical energy knocked all those it hit off their feet. They sparkled and fizzled, not with electrical energy but magical, and just enough to hold them in place.

"That will not work for long," Master Rackson breathed. "Go!"

"Come on guys!" De grabbed Mo's hand and the four of them ran as fast as they could up the rest of the hill, leaving the Racksons outside as they entered the manor to face A.G. herself.

The foyer of the manor matched the outside of it: dark, creepy, and foreboding. The Elementals filed in the door after De and sheltered themselves behind him; all of them obviously terrified.

"Where is she?" Mo whispered.

"How should I know?" De hissed back.

"Ain't you the leader? Shouldn't you know this stuff?" Rod asked.

"Yes! I mean, no! I mean...I kinda figured she'd be waiting for us at the front door..." De admitted.

"Some leader," M muttered.

"Ok fine! We're just gonna have to split up and find her," De said.

"Split up?!" For once all three of his fellow Elementals agreed on something, and that something was that De had lost his mind.

"Yes split up. This is a huge house; it'll take us forever to search everywhere all together. M and I will go upstairs. Mo, you go right towards the guest rooms. Rod, you head to the left by the kitchen and stuff, that way you'll be near some water if you need it. If anybody sees any traces of her don't fight her! Just holler and we'll come meet you. Ten minutes and we meet back here, ok?"

"Fine by me," M nodded and started walking towards the stairs.

"I guess so..." Mo agreed. He plugged a pocket charger into the laser hand he "borrowed" from Don.

"I just hope I don't get killed before I can yell," Rod said.

"Well let's get this going," De said, and everyone went their separate ways.

"Ok, I'm gonna go towards Master Rackson's study and Rose's room. You head towards the other bedrooms," De suggested.

"Cool," M said. He started to walk off towards his location but turned back. "De? Do you really think we can do this?"

De looked earnestly at M. "I really don't know, but I know we have to try. If we don't everything we did and everyone who has been lost..." His mind went back to his foster parents. "...would have died for nothing."

M nodded. "You know, you are pretty good in these situations. I guess I see why the other guys wanted you in charge."

"Was that a compliment?! From you? Okay now I'm scared." De was only half joking.

"Don't get used to it. I could still kick your butt. I'll prove it after we figure out where A.G. is." M said back.

De laughed in spite of himself. "Keep thinking that little man, don't you remember our sparring match down in the..." Then it hit him. M realized it as well.

"The bunker!" They both said. They ran back down the stairs and called for Rod and Mo. The two came running from their sides of the manor, Rod with a trail of water behind him and Mo holding the laser hand.

"What? Did you find her?" he asked.

"We think she's in the bunker where we train, it's the safest place in the house and the only place you can get to from almost anywhere in here," M explained, thinking of all the secret passageways to it.

"Well what are we waiting on?" Rod asked. "Let's....whoa!!" He leapt backwards and dropped the water he was controlling when he dodged a small green laser blast that came up from under his feet. More small, concentrated blasts shot upwards from below them, sending the Elementals running to a corner of the room.

"Well there's our answer!" De said "Come on guys!" De kicked open the door that led down to the basement bunker and the four boys ran down the stairs and into the room that they usually used for training. The second they all got in A.G. fired the Orange Scepter at them again, blasting a good part of the stairs away and scattering the heroes across the room.

"So, let's get this plan going!" M said. Fear was strong in his voice, but despite it (or perhaps because of it) he started firing off the strongest electricity he could muster at A.G. Mo tried blasting her with the laser hand, but the battle trained android easily dodged both of their attacks and continued to launch her own. The power of the Orange Scepter rocked and rumbled the fortified room, but not even it could destroy anything inside of it.

"Be looking for an opening!" De told Rod. He then jumped into the fray as well, throwing flame after flame at the android.

"Yeah...sure..." Rod groaned, watching the villain's movements for any type of weakness.

Lucas launched his hand (currently shaped like a blade) straight forward. It extended right into one android's chest and came out the other side. He withdrew it and his target fell to the ground. He jogged up the hill to help his father and aunt tag team one of the Battle Robots. Master Rackson had aimed his powers at the blade hand of a robot they had already defeated and launched it at the oncoming robot. It impaled the robot's side, but the machine kept trying to squash the three of them under its feet.

"I would have never believed that we would be doing

this again!" Master Rackson said to his sister over the sound of the stomping robot.

Rose smiled and looked at the sky. She opened her arms wide and allowed the energy from the bright sunny sky to charge her body. Her power to channel solar energy made her attacks much more powerful, which was needed for her to hold the many androids that surrounded them at bay. She reached out and started punching at the androids nearest her, but even she was having trouble keeping up. Lucas looked at the onslaught of androids approaching his aunt and got an idea.

"I hope this works..." he focused his own power, and willed his spare hand to take the form of one of the android's laser hands. To his surprise, it worked. He giddily fired off a few lasers to back the androids off of his aunt before joining his father.

Master Rackson was working on helping himself. Once his first plan didn't work he withdrew the gigantic blade from the robots side, but the focus he had to keep on the giant blade left him open to attack. Lucas ran towards him to fire laser blasts at the androids around his father.

"What are you doing?!" Lucas yelled at Master Rackson, who was still magically levitating the giant blade.

"Distract the Battle Robot!" was all Master Rackson breathed back. Rose heard her brother's request and after kicking the four androids nearest her away, ran to the giant robot. She hit its legs with everything she had, distracting it long enough for Master Rackson to slice the Battle Robot with its own blade; bringing it to a quick stop.

Once Lucas stopped the last of the androids with his laser hands, he changed back to normal and the exhausted family stood in the middle of their yard.

"We gotta...whew...we gotta get inside," said Rose. Lucas and Master Rackson nodded, but as they neared their home Master Rackson was struck from behind by another blast. As his sister and son helped him to his feet they all turned around to see what must have been another dozen or so androids and another Battle Robot stomping from the city. All three Racksons cursed their luck and looked at each other.

"I hope the others are doing better inside..." Lucas commented.

The intensity of De's flaming breath chased A.G. away from blasting Mo with the Scepter. "Are you ok?" he asked Mo.

"I'm ok, just go after her!" he held his side but motioned for De to keep fighting. The battle was taking its toll on all of them. Rod had been singed a couple times by A.G.'s blasts for trying to get too close to her at the wrong times, M's electric blasts were steadily losing strength, and Mo was purely exhausted. Even De was barely hanging on to the fight, but the evil android hadn't tired yet. She fired another Orange Scepter blast at De, and the Elemental only barely got out of the way in time. The blast hit the wall behind him and rocked the room again.

"This is getting hopeless!" M told De.

"We can't stop! We have to get rid of this thing!" De said back. He threw a couple more flames at A.G. to get the android to focus on him, which worked. The android ran towards De and not even bothering to fire the thing again; hit him with the Scepter across the chest. The metal in the weapon would surely have rendered any normal person unconscious, but thanks to the Elementals' increased endurance it only knocked the breath out of De and knocked him to the floor.

Even with this added endurance the Elementals were being pushed to their limits: Mo laid helplessly on what remained of the stairs; his laser hand damaged beyond repair by A.G.'s attacks, and M struggled to get to his feet to help De. Neither of them were a sufficient enough distraction from Rod limping to the house at the back of the bunker. He had remembered it suddenly just a few moments ago, and hoped to all of the Mystics it was still there. A.G. chased after him, firing her lasers at him just as he flung the front door open. Laser blasts rocked the storage space as Rod searched the area frantically. Eventually he found it: the mop bucket that he used to fight the dummy in training, still half full of water. He smiled at his awesome luck, and pushed the bucket outside the area. A.G. was nearly on top of the Water Elemental, and in a reflex he flung the water onto A.G.

The android stumbled, but only for a moment. Thankfully that moment was all Rod needed. He sucked the water off of A.G. and splashed her with it again and again, creating a torrent of liquid that made it difficult for the android to see her attacker. The others moved as fast as they could towards Rod to help him, but by this time A.G. had started firing off small laser blasts from the Orange Scepter in every direction and they had to slow down even further to avoid being hit. One of the blasts caught Rod in the chest, and the warrior went flying backwards into the house.

"NO!" the other three yelled. A.G backed away and wiped her face clear of Rod's last attack. It wasn't until the Elementals poured into the house that she saw her handiwork, and actually laughed. It was a cold, distant sort of sound that frightened the Elementals even more than the possibility that

Rod may be no more. De grabbed Rod by the shoulders and gave him a shake, but he didn't move.

"Are you ok? Say something!" Mo begged.

"Come on dude, wake up," De patted Rod's face to try to wake him.

M saw that Rod wasn't budging, and instead of trying to revive him, he went straight for the cackling android. He ran towards her, throwing as many electric blasts her way as he could. She dodged a few of the blasts, but a couple hit her head on. Instead of fizzling or even slowing down though, it seemed that M had only angered the android.

"You have seen the power of the Pru Empire, and yet you still foolishly choose to fight. Explain."

"You gotta go down, that's why!" M shot an electric bolt so powerful it shut off one of the fluorescent lights between him and A.G. as it traveled. The blast actually made A.G. stumble, to her surprise and M's. The other two Elementals, however, where still focused on their fallen comrade.

"Come on get up! After all that trash you talked, you better not be dead!" Mo's voice started condescending, but he soon became much more serious. "Please..." he stopped talking and just looked away. De panted and sputtered, unable to believe what he was seeing, and with a shaking hand gently laid Rod's head back on the floor.

"Is he...?" Mo asked.

De felt Rod's chest. When it rose just slightly and sunk De shook his head. "He's alive. I guess I was right...that should've taken him out but he's okay," he smiled in pure relief for a moment before turning to Mo. "That means-" De's words were drowned out by another of A.G.'s chilling laughs. He and

Mo peered out of the house to see M being lifted up off the ground by A.G. with the Orange Scepter leveled at his head.

"You will not survive this, Elemental. You will know firsthand the wrath of the Pru Empire, and you will regret this day," she threatened. The Orange Scepter began to glow with the energy of the forthcoming attack, while De and Mo scrambled to their feet to try to avoid another casualty. The Orange Scepter might not be able to kill them, but they'd hate to see what sort of damage it would do that close...

And then several things happened at once.

M used every last bit of his remaining power to fire one last electric blast at A.G.'s hand holding the Orange Scepter. At such close range and with so much energy put into it, the attack knocked the Scepter from her hand and it flew into the wall on her right side. A.G. threw M into one of the fortified walls and he hit the ground, the impact and his own exhaustion kept him from moving again. A.G. dove after the Scepter just as De was running and doing the same. The few milliseconds A.G. wasted getting rid of M gave De the opportunity to snatch the scepter first. He threw the Scepter to Mo and as he did so A.G. sent a laser blast at De. He went sliding across the floor from the force of the blast, his chest smoking from the point where A.G.'s eye blasts hit him. Mo, in a fit of surprising bravery, didn't run as the android rounded on him, but reflexively aimed the Scepter at her. From the orb at the top of the Scepter came a blast of freezing air rather than the lasers that A.G. had been firing. The cold energy connected with A.G. and encased the android in a thick layer of ice.

Mo's jaw dropped in shock as he approached the frozen machine. De got up, still clutching his chest and approached Mo. He looked from A.G. to the Orange Scepter and back to his comrade before he spoke a word.

"How did you do that?!" De asked.

"I-I don't know..." Mo admitted. "I didn't know I could do that..." he and De looked at the still frozen solid A.G. in utter disbelief.

"Hand me the Scepter, Mo," De said suddenly.

"What? No, you can't use it; she'll thaw out!"

"Just hand me the Scepter. I have an idea," De said. Mo did as he was told and handed the powerful weapon to the Fire Elemental. Instead of aiming the orb of the weapon like Mo did, however, he turned it upside down in his hands and took a swipe at one of A.G.'s frozen appendages.

"What are you doing?!" Mo screamed as A.G.'s frozen arm fell to the ground.

"Doing what needs to be done," De said flatly. Images from their journey thus far flashed in his mind with each swipe at the android. The destroyed cities, the broken families, the storeowner, his foster parents...

"Wait, I want a swing!" Mo said.

Before De could hand the weapon to Mo for his shot at the android, he drove it directly into her chest, activating some sort of last minute defense mechanism. The laser blast that came from A.G.'s eyes was wide and strong enough to break through the ice and knock the still exhausted De and Mo unconscious; leaving them on the floor of the bunker with their unconscious comrades and the five pieces of A.G.

Review Day

Three Months Later

"Bye Dad! Bye Lauryn!" Mo called happily to his family as he left the house. Aside from a few bad nightmares reminding him; he had completely moved on from the A.G. ordeal.

"Wait, where are you going?" Prof. Peters emerged from their living room at the sound of his son's voice. In the time since his release from prison Prof. Peters' had become much more interested in keeping up with his son's location, especially since he finally knew about his son's Elemental-ness.

"I'm going to the Racksons' house, Dad. We have training today," Mo felt like he had to have told his father this at least four times already.

"Why are you training? A.G. is gone; her body is where no one will ever find it-"

"I wish you had just destroyed that thing," Mo said with a shudder.

"You know that was impossible. I did the next best thing." The professor's design worked a little too well, and the metal that made up A.G.'s body, though in pieces, was still resilient to any type of full destruction. Rather than take any chances both Master Rackson and Prof. Peters decided to simply place the pieces in a remote location and tell no one where they placed them. "Don't change the subject, Morgan. Why do you have to go to training?" Prof. Peters said.

"We still got stuff to do, Dad! I thought you understood this, I mean when I told you-"

"It's not that I have a problem with you being...an

Elemental. It's just that I want you to be safe," Prof. Peters explained.

"Henry let him go, he'll be fine," Lauryn had finally joined the two in the space between the living room door and the front door.

"But he does not-" Prof. Peters began.

"Bye Morgan, be safe," Lauryn interrupted and opened the door for him.

"Thanks! See you!" Mo said as he walked out of the door, but not before he hugged both Lauryn and his father, leaving the old professor once again speechless.

"Wonderful. It is great to see all of you again," Master Rackson beamed around his study at De, M, Rod, Mo, Rose and Don. We have two very important matters to discuss today-"

"Very important," Rod agreed. Aside from the scar on his chest from A.G.'s Orange Scepter blast, he too, had moved on from the journey to defeat A.G. He was enjoying several perks of being on the other side of the law, as was obvious in the expensive clothes and complex new design in his braids.

"Yea yea, we all know about your sister discovering her powers. I wanna know what the other news is. Some new crazy invention on the loose?" M sat up on his chair and grinned. With A.G. gone his parents had demanded he focus on his schoolwork again. M complained that school was boring after having saved the world, but his parents believed that if he could save the world then he should focus on saving his grade point average.

"No Maurice we will not," Master Rackson laughed. "We will, however, be deciding on something simi-"

"Am I late?" Lucas Rackson rushed into the room and

looked around anxiously. Even though he was a part of the generation and welcome in Rackson Manor he was still unable to live under one roof with his father. Rose decided to help him get a small apartment in Cirix until things were better.

"Yep, but sit down anyway," Rose said with a warm smile. Lucas nodded and grabbed the nearest empty chair.

"I suppose I had better finish before I am interrupted again," Master Rackson said, laughing once again. This time, the rest of the room joined in. "The first order of business is that now that you all have accomplished your first major task as Elementals, you must have a generation name."

"How about the Justice Squad?" Don suggested and Mo nodded enthusiastically. Though he was still disappointed he couldn't watch A.G.'s defeat he was finally off crutches and was back to his normal happy self. "It sounds-"

"It sounds stolen. What show did that come from?" De interrupted. His life had probably changed most: thanks to generous donations from grateful citizens he was almost ready to move out of Rackson Manor, Master Rackson had spoken with several school officials to try to get him placed in a school, and best of all the monks let him keep the convertible. Rod laughed across from him.

"Well...it's not...not really at least..." Don actually seemed a little disappointed.

"Well why do we need a name anyway? A.G.'s gone, the androids are spare parts and best of all my parole is up. We did what we needed to do," Rod said.

"This is the end of your journey to defeat A.G., yes. But as a team of Elementals your times together are just beginning," Master Rackson assured him.

"We still have to find those Prudence kids, and bring

them in," De pointed out.

"Plus help the country rebuild now that the androids are pretty much all gone," M added. After taking a week or so to fully recover all eight of them began the long process of rounding up all the leftover androids and taking them down.

"Yes, revel in your accomplishments and rejoice in your achievements, for you have made your mark on history by ending the rule of the tyrant A.G. You new Elementals of the fifth generation...G5..." Master Rackson paused to test the reactions to this new name.

"I like it," Lucas said quietly. The other four Elementals agreed.

"Well then G5, congratulations, the road will only continue higher from here," Master Rackson finished.

"So what is the other matter?" Don asked.

"My sister! She's downstairs waiting on us. She has got to learn how to control her powers so she can stop turning our house into a wind tunnel!" Rod said.

"I thought you said that we don't need to do anything else?" De grinned.

"We don't have to do anything else...after this," Rod clarified.

"What's the matter Rod? Can't handle living with an Elemental woman?" Rose teased.

"It's Rod's sister though, Rose. She's not a woman," M said.

"What do you know about women anyway?" De asked.

"More than you! You don't know anything! You barely know where you live!" M shot back.

"My dear Maurice. You could know all the facts in the

world and you would still never-" Master Rackson began, but Rose shot him a dirty look. He grinned and said no more. "Perhaps we should just go see Jasmin." Master Rackson opened the door and headed for the stairs, with his son and his sister right behind him.

"Good idea. It would probably be this kid's first time seeing a girl." Rod said, pointing at Mo as he got up.

"Shut up, Rod!" Mo said back. He waited until Rod was out of the door before he muttered more insults to himself.

"What did you say?!" Rod yelled from the hallway.

"Let it go man! We don't have time for this!" De reached out to stop Rod from walking back into the room. Mo ran and hid behind Don (which was still fairly easy to do) while Rod continued to threaten him and both Mo and Don argued back.

"Oh just let them fight!" M said, which caused De to yell at him.

As the five boys continued to argue and yell at each other it was hard to believe that it was their bravery and teamwork that had stopped the evil A.G.'s reign of terror and brought peace back to their land. Regardless of their dysfunctional nature, however, G5 and their ally would go down as true heroes; those worthy of carrying the title of Elemental.

The adventure continues…

RETURN OF A.G.

Two years after the Elementals defeated the rogue Guardroid A.G., life for them has changed dramatically. Their generation has grown and their fame has increased, but one thing remains the same: they're still having to learn to deal with each other. The stakes couldn't be higher this time around, as it comes to their attention that someone is trying to bring back A.G. and using one of their teammates to do it. Will the heroes be able to stop A.G.'s return and find out who is the traitor among them?

Return of A.G. continues the tale of the Elementals and takes their journey through unexpected turns. With a host of new characters and locations, the world of Colorius has never felt more real. By the end of this story you'll be even more addicted to the world M. Haynes has created.

Keep up with the Elemental series and the author at www.mhaynes.org!

ABOUT THE AUTHOR

M. Haynes has been writing since the age of nine, and what started as a fun hobby soon became a full-fledged passion. Legend of the Orange Scepter began his journey to create a series in his favorite genre that focused on characters of color. He hopes that his work will be a stepping stone to more equal representation overall and a source of pride for youth.

M. Haynes is a son of the south: Tennessee born, Mississippi raised, and he currently lives and teaches in Georgia.

Made in the USA
Columbia, SC
05 February 2018